For Denise,

LOVE.

LIZ LEIBY

"Gouda
vibes
only"

(signature)

To Allen, whose love healed a part of me that I didn't know needed to be healed.
And to Marie, my dearest friend during the darkest time

---

*E*xcept for a layer of dust, my grandparents' cabin looks exactly the way it did three years ago. Standing in the doorway, suitcase in hand, tears well in my eyes for at least the fourth time today. Grammy's crocheted blanket is still draped across the back of the floral couch where I spent countless Christmases waiting for Santa. My framed childhood artwork still decorates the walls, and the tall black chimney still commands the space as if the entire cabin were made for the wood stove instead of the other way around. My boots echo on the hardwood floor, and I inhale deeply, searching for the familiar scents of my childhood: woodsmoke and lavender. I drop my suitcase and sneeze into my elbow.

"Sorry, we haven't been up here to dust since last year. We skipped our usual summer trip. I know it's bad." My older sister, Charleigh, marches in from outside and sets down a box on the couch. A puff of dust billows up. We both lean back, covering our noses with sleeved hands, coughing and wafting the dust away from our faces.

"It's fine," I say. "I kind of sprung this on you."

Last week when my bank account told me I couldn't afford to live in a hotel any longer, I called Charleigh and asked if I could use the cabin. Considering we haven't spoken in three years her response was generous, but I've recently left my boyfriend of twelve years, so maybe it was just pity.

"I can start on dinner if you want to get the rest of the stuff from the car. I think there's just one box in the trunk. You didn't bring much."

"I don't have much," I say over my shoulder as I head back outside.

I stare into the open trunk of Charleigh's SUV. She was right —there is only one item left: a travel-size storage case stuffed with art supplies, mostly paints and brushes. It's not even close to the full extent of my collection, but it was all I could convince myself to bring. In reality, I own more art supplies than clothes. I paint for a living, and most of my clothes are covered in paint anyway. I need supplies more than I need clothes. I used to find it all so amusing, but now it makes my stomach hurt.

For as long as I can remember, I've been able to look at a canvas and see exactly what it needs to be. Any paint color I choose, I know what it needs to be paired with, the kind of strokes and depth needed to create the picture in my mind. When forced to do the mundane, groceries and dishes, I'm mentally composing the next painting, my fingers itching all the while, desperate to get back to my brushes. I've never known a day without an idea, without the swirl of colors and the siren call of creativity, so I've never known a life without my art.

But six months ago, when my life fell apart, something changed. There are no ideas, no pictures in my head, and my fingers don't itch. I know what's happened to me, but no one else does—not my agent, not my family. I haven't been brave enough to speak the truth out loud.

I can't paint anymore.

I drag the supply box closer to me, unlatching it. Everything got jostled during my flight, so I carefully rearrange it. It seems silly to have all these supplies and no ideas. It feels like a betrayal, but I arrange them anyway. When everything is just so, I pick up the thinnest brush, running my fingertip over the bristles. They tickle my skin and spring back into place. My body relaxes at the memory of this feeling. I've felt it a thousand times. I catch a whiff of turpentine and tears prick my eyes. What color did I last use on this brush? What painting did it create? My chest squeezes, and before I can stop myself I snap the small brush in two.

A rush of shame and horror washes over me, but the urge to rid myself of these supplies is spontaneous and fierce and I'm powerless against it. They taunt me by just existing, and I want to be rid of them. I hurl the next two brushes on the ground, hard enough that they bounce a little after hitting the gravel.

When I empty the box of brushes, purging myself of every traitorous tool, I start in on a paint tube and squeeze it all out onto the ground. Watching the color drain from the tube is so satisfying a sudden giddiness hits me, and I laugh a maniacal, foreign laugh I don't even recognize.

"Hey, do you want—?"

My head snaps back in Charleigh's direction as I hide the empty paint tube behind my back, face burning. She flies off the porch only to stop short, assessing the damage around me. At my feet is a graveyard of broken brushes and wasted paint.

"Oh my god. What the hell are you doing?"

I slump on the edge of the car trunk as my legs turn to jelly.

What was I doing? I've never done a thing like that in my life. Those are expensive supplies, and if I need them again . . .

Who am I kidding? I can't paint anymore.

My jaw works, trying to form words, but I have no idea how to explain myself.

"I'm going to ask the obvious question: how will you paint? Don't you have clients?"

"No." My voice is strained, held tight by the embarrassment of being caught.

My agent, Jackie, has been pushing off my clients for me. She said artists at my level can afford to take some time off, and she was right. I did okay for a few months. Jackie probably hoped I'd be painting again by now, but I've turned down every opportunity that's come my way in the past six months. I don't think I can say no for much longer, but I don't think I'm ready to say yes either.

"I'll clean it up," I say, but I realize, she's already done it when I see Charleigh's full hands.

She sighs the way I imagine she sighs at her daughter when she's done something she shouldn't. "I need to get back to dinner," she says and walks into the house.

We have no idea how to be around each other right now. The hour-and-twenty-minute car ride from Denver was the strangest mix of comfortable and tense. We were close our whole lives—that is until about three years ago—but we haven't spoken since the incident after my grandparents' funeral. So now we dance around each other, our conversations both stilted and familiar, unable to find the balance between our bond and our brokenness.

I smear a tiny pyramid of paint further into the gravel with my shoe. I want to feel guilty that I ruined my supplies, but my art abandoned me. It left me during a time I needed it most. I left my boyfriend, and my art left me.

When I step into the cabin, the smell of the groceries we brought with us greets me: onions, garlic, and that unnamed meat flavor only found in jars of red sauce. Charleigh tends to multiple pots on the stove in the small kitchen just off the entrance. Grammy used to joke the kitchen needed a chandelier it was so close to the front door. Grampy once tried to give her one made from antlers, but she refused to hang it.

"I think I've got a lead on a car for you," Charleigh says, bustling around in the kitchen.

Charleigh's always been better at the practical details. She's the kind of person who plans her outfits and gets her hair cut every three months on the dot. She has drawer organizers for her clothes, utensils, and office supplies. I'm the kind of person who loses the drink I was just holding, never shows up to an event less than five minutes late, and most definitely did not think of transportation when I packed up my life to move here.

"Oh. Thank you. And thanks for cooking," I say and amble into the kitchen to get a glass of water.

"No problem," Charleigh says, dumping cooked noodles into a colander and then transferring it all to a large bowl. She pours the warmed jar sauce onto them and mixes it up, scooping some into a bowl for me.

"Do you want to eat in the sunroom?" I ask, taking the bowl and picking out forks for us. There's a small table for two in there, nestled against one of the walls of windows. Grammy and Grampy would break out an old card table when we came to visit so we could all sit in the same room. Eventually the card table broke and we just ate off TV trays while sitting on the couches.

"I don't feel like warming it," Charleigh says with a shrug.

I follow her into the living room, both of us curling up on opposite ends of the couch.

Growing up, I thought our cabin was special, that my grandfather built it from the ground up. It turns out all the cabins on this road are built by some cabin company and identical, with an open-plan kitchen and living room and either two bedrooms off to the sides or one at the back. There is one space that makes our cabin unique though: the sunroom. Grampy had it built specially for Grammy. Attached to the back of the cabin and enclosed entirely in glass, the sunroom has a full view of the woods behind the house. Charleigh and I used to sleep in there when we came to visit. Grampy would pull out the couch bed for us, and even when we were teenagers and way too old for it we'd snuggle in our sleeping bags and stare through the glass at the night sky, counting stars until we fell asleep. I glance at it now, darkened and dusty, and a heaviness settles in my bones. Charleigh and I are long past those days.

The silence between us stretches awkward and uncomfortable. I can think of a million things to say, but none of them seem right.

"So," Charleigh says after taking a big bite of noodles, "what happened?"

"Ben and Blair have been sleeping together," I say, twirling my fork.

Charleigh's jaw goes slack and she claps her hand over her mouth. There's a painful tightness in my throat, and swallowing my next bite takes a Herculean effort.

"Blair? As in, your best friend Blair?" she asks behind her hand.

"Yep," I say, as cool as I can, but my body starts to tremble. Remembering the way my boyfriend and best friend sat me down and told me they had to tell me something, my hunger turns to nausea.

"Jesus, Mara. For how long?" There's pain in Charleigh's voice, as if we share two pieces of one heart and her piece is breaking in tandem with mine.

"I didn't ask."

They started to tell me everything, but I stopped them. I said I didn't care, that I hoped they had a happy life. I packed a bag and left, only later going back for my things. At the time I felt numb, but it didn't take long for the weight of my grief to imprison me in a hotel room for a month.

"When did you find out?"

"April."

It feels like so long ago, and sometimes like it was yesterday.

I carry my untouched dinner to the kitchen and root around in the lower cabinets where Grammy always kept the Tupperware.

"April? What the hell, Mara—why didn't you say anything?" Charleigh's voice is part anger, part shock, and full of disappointment. She practically leaps from the couch, all but slamming her bowl on the counter. "It's September—actually, it's almost October! Why am I just now learning about this?"

"We weren't exactly on speaking terms." I dump the noodles and sauce from my bowl into a container and seal it up, sticking it in the fridge.

"What have you been doing for nearly six months? Where have you been living?" She catches my arm as I try to walk past her out of the kitchen.

"I've been in therapy the past six months and living in a hotel," I say, the weight in my bones suddenly too much to bear. "Listen, I'm really tired and I'm going to go unpack."

She swallows hard, her brow furrowed. But she nods and releases me.

After my flight this morning from Philly, reuniting with my sister after not speaking for three years and moving into my dead grandparents' cabin, my heart feels like a freshly picked scab. I don't know what I thought today would be like, but I hoped I'd finally have a sense of peace.

All I have is the absence of people I miss.

The phantom scents of my grandparents linger in their room, a mixture of fire smoke, Budweiser, and lavender. Their absence sits heavy in the pit of my stomach—a grief that looms larger now I'm back in this cabin in their old bedroom.

Nothing in this room has changed. The bed frame is the same old wooden one my grandparents used, and while the quilt is unchanged, when I press on the bed it gives—a sign the mattress got a much-needed upgrade. The dresser against the wall isn't any different either, and I run my hand along the dark wood remembering the objects that used to live here: small framed photos of Charleigh and me as kids, necklaces and rings bursting from my grandmother's jewelry box, and all the random objects that came from my grandfather's pockets—coins, acorns, and sticks of gum. What I wouldn't give to be ten again, exploring the treasures of my grandparents' lives. I twist the turquoise and silver ring around my middle finger. It's one of the few treasures I still have.

Turning back to the suitcase on the bed, I dump the contents into one large pile of clothing. I rush through the process of putting clothes away, tucking each item into the drawers with no discernible pattern. Charleigh would probably have something to say about my lack of a system, but I've never been the organized one. She was the A+ student who graduated valedictorian and went to grad school while working her financial planning job and raising a kid. She's one of the top financial managers at her firm now and has as many certifications as she qualifies for. I was a C student who thrived only in art class, graduating by the skin of my teeth. My family was thrilled when I sold my first painting, I think because they were worried I wouldn't be able to do anything else. But even as I dove headfirst into my career, agent secured and art selling as often as it was displayed, my parents weren't fully convinced I'd be okay. They were supportive but never stopped wringing their hands over my career choice.

Which is one of the many reasons I've downplayed my loss. My agent and parents know I've got a little creative block, but they don't know how bad it is. It's been years now since anyone worried about my career, which has been successful by all standards, and I don't need their concern adding to the weight on my chest.

I rezip my suitcase and drag it off the bed, but as I do I hear the slide of an object in the front pocket. I open the closet door—which is just wide enough to fit the suitcase—and stuff it inside. My parents used to complain about how small the closets were, but as kids Charleigh and I found them to be the perfect size for hide-and-seek.

I reach into the front pocket and pull out a shirt, freezing when I realize it doesn't technically belong to me. It belongs to Ben, my boyfriend.

My *ex*-boyfriend.

I thought I left all the clothes that remind me of him in my storage unit, but I must have missed this one. The shirt is soft, worn from repeated washes and time. It's dark green and has the name of the college we went to stamped across the chest. I run my hand over the faded letters, breath hitching. It was the first shirt of his I claimed as my own.

I hoped by coming to Colorado I could escape the city filled with memories of Ben. I hoped I could get inspired, find my art and identity again, but I feel more lost here than I did in that hotel room in Philadelphia.

My chin wobbles, my lips quiver, and with no warning tears spill down my cheeks. I scoot to the bedroom door, leaning against it for support, and bury my face in the shirt. It absorbs the grief of being back in this cabin again, my worries about never being able to paint again, the anguish of my broken relationship with Charleigh, and all the sadness that's clung to me for months.

When I finally crawl into bed, eyes swollen and aching, I take the shirt with me, cradling it like a precious blanket. I don't miss Ben so much as I miss my old life—the one where I wasn't haunted by all the missing pieces of me.

2

*G*rowing up in Texas, Colorado was always a wonder to me. The mountains captivated me. How could there be so much to see, so much beauty, when Texas was so flat and dull?

As Charleigh and I drive into town this morning, I feel like a child again in awe of the mountains, overwhelmed by their ever-looming presence and power. The twenty-minute drive is one of my favorites, filled with colors I've captured again and again on canvas, and I still never seem to get it just right.

Copper Springs is one of many former mining towns nestled in the mountains with one central, two-lane road sandwiched between dozens of stores and restaurants. There's ample bike and car parking, and since tourist season is almost over, finding a spot isn't too hard. I wasn't keen to leave the cabin since we've only been here for two days, but Charleigh insisted.

This is how it's always been with her. Charleigh in charge.

"So I thought we could start at Gino's for groceries," my sister says, "and then we could get sandwiches at the cheese shop." She's stepping out onto the thin ice between us, offering her hand so we can find steadier ground.

I don't accept her offering. "I'm going to be hungry for more than just cheese. Why can't we go to Park's Deli?"

"The Gouda Times Bistro *is* Park's Deli. The owner, Arjun, bought it three years ago and expanded. He made some changes, and now there's tons of cheese and local jams and wines. Trust me, it's a great spot. And Arjun is easy on the eyes."

"Did you just say Gouda Times Bistro?" I intentionally ignore her comment about the owner. The last thing I'm interested in right now is a relationship or hookup or anything of the sort.

"I know, I know. But seriously, the guy knows his cheese."

I sigh as I drag myself out the car.

I used to love coming into town with Grammy. We'd come empty-handed and hungry and leave bellies bursting and arms heavy with goodies. Now, as Charleigh and I walk down the familiar street, I only recognize a handful of stores. My throat feels thick with longing for the way things used to be.

We pass a clothing store I recall being filled with touristy merch and knickknacks, a smoothie place I've never seen before, and a new candle shop. The next store stops me dead in my tracks. It definitely was not here three years ago. My fingers brush against the window of the store like a child who's just seen a puppy begging to be adopted.

"Do you wanna go in?" Charleigh asks.

"I don't need anything." *I won't use anything.*

"Even though you destroyed your supplies yesterday?"

"I have some left," I lie.

My body has an agenda of its own, though, and almost against my own will I open the door to The Artist's Outlet, an art supplies store.

"Hey," Charleigh calls after me. "I'm going to Gino's, but I'll meet you at the cheese place in thirty, okay?"

The door closes behind me with a jingle.

The store is quiet except for the soft K-pop coming through the speakers. It's chilly in here, and I stuff my hands in my pockets. I wander the aisles, stopping occasionally to admire the stock of colored pencils, the collection of oil paints, and the variety of canvas sizes and sketchbook options. I'm impressed by the stock for such a small town. Whoever the owner is, they know their stuff. I peer around the store but don't see anyone, not even at the register.

The row of aisles opens into a small seating area. Two over-stuffed chairs face a propane fireplace. On a small table between the chairs is a quirky vintage lamp circa the fifties or sixties. I've never seen a seating area in an art supplies store before, but I'm not surprised. That's Colorado. Quaint and quirky.

My breath sticks in my chest when my eyes land on the main feature: a large oil painting hanging above the fireplace. I freeze, my heart racing.

This is one of my paintings.

"Do you like it?" A cheery female voice comes from behind me.

I twist around, matching the voice to one of the most eclectically dressed people I've ever seen. A woman about my age, wearing a lavender turtleneck layered under a bright mustard T-shirt, stands nearby. She's wrapped herself in a crocheted shawl the exact shade of white as her knee-length skirt. Purple tights, gray socks, and black ballet flats complete the outfit.

"Like it?" I ask, not sure exactly what she's referring to. The seating area? The painting?

"The painting. It's an M. North painting," the girl says, her smile widening, brightening, just a little more. She points to the painting, and I whip back around to face it.

I know I need to respond, but how can I speak when I can't even breathe? "I, uh...yeah. I do. Like it."

"The artist is my favorite. M. North. Have you heard of them?"

"I have, actually."

I know M. North because I am M. North. The only people in the world who know this are Ben, my agent Jackie, and my immediate family. My friend circle shrank to just Ben after college, and I never got involved in a local community with other artists, so I didn't have anyone to tell. I've attended all my own exhibitions as a stranger in the crowd. My agent handles all my interviews and PR. When people ask what I do for a living, they're satisfied with my simple answer: "I'm an artist." If anyone asks if they know my work, I always tell them no.

"Oh! You must be into the art scene. They're not as well-known outside of it, but inside the art world the identity of M. North is the decade's biggest mystery and best-kept secret. They're like Banksy. Anyway. My favorite."

I smile, facing this odd, overly friendly girl. This is a first for me, meeting a fan. I didn't know I had any. People have asked for commissions over the years, but they're mostly collectors— people who have entire rooms dedicated to art, my piece just one among many.

"This is my favorite of theirs." She gestures to the painting. "It's called 'Wilderness.' It reminds me of the woods around here." She points to the windows. "These trees, these mountains. They captured the feeling of being here. A little uncanny when you think about it, like maybe they've been here. Although Colorado is a big place. Could have been anywhere, but what if it were here in Copper Springs? That would be really exciting! Sorry, I'm rambling. Here's why I love this painting: you know how sometimes you look at a painting and it just makes you think of one word, one feeling? This word is 'belonging.' Like I belong HERE, in these woods, in this moment. I don't know. It's hard to describe, you know."

"It is, but I think you described it perfectly."

Her energy is contagious and a little overwhelming. Part of me wants to run away, but the other part wants to lean in. Her face is filled with childlike wonder. It moves me, seeing her so enraptured with something I created. I long for my brushes and time alone to paint, only for the yearning to transform to anguish the way a wave crashes and is no longer a wave.

I keep forgetting that part of me is dead. A chill runs up my arms, followed by a heaviness that urges me to sit down. I lean against one of the chairs for support.

"I'm sorry, I just talked your ear off and I don't even know your name, and you don't know mine. I'm Dany. With a Y. Which is short for Danielle, which is actually my middle name. My first name is Ruth, but you can call me Dany," she says without taking a breath, extending her hand toward me.

"Mara. Mara West." I take her hand, offering a small smile. It isn't much, but she seems to accept it with enthusiasm.

"Dany Kirk, like the captain."

"Live long and prosper." The corners of my lips tug, a smile trying to break through the crushing melancholy.

An explosive laugh bursts out of Dany's mouth. "I like you already. I think we'll be friends. Please tell me you're not a tourist who's only in town for the week."

Her joy is infectious, and despite not wanting to leave the

cabin today, I'm starting to think it wasn't such a bad idea after all.

"Not a tourist," I confirm. "I live here now, in a cabin about fifteen minutes up Pine Road."

"I know those cabins! Is yours the one with the yellow door? I know the people who live in the cabins with the green door and blue door, but I don't know the yellow door owner, so that has to be you. Right?"

"That's the one."

"Ah! So cool! Did you just buy it? I didn't see a for-sale sign."

"It belonged to my grandparents, but they died a few years back and left the cabin to me and my sister. Usually, my sister and her family use it for holidays and such. I just got out of a long-term relationship, so I'm here for a bit while I figure out my life."

As soon as the words are out of my mouth, I cringe inside. I definitely overshared. She's going to think I'm a wet blanket, too depressing to talk to anymore. I take a fleeting look at the exit, eager to leave.

"Oh, Mara. I'm so sorry, but it is obvious that we were destined to meet today and become friends, and we're going to be fast friends, I can just tell."

My oversharing being met with kindness and eagerness for friendship is a relief, and I let it sink into my bones. I press my lips into a thin smile. I can't promise friendship to her, but she should know I appreciate her words.

"Are you an artist?" she asks. "I know you're in an art supplies store, but you'd be surprised. We get all types in here."

"Yes, I paint. Well . . . it's complicated," I say, not sure how to explain myself and not wanting to.

"I knew it. Plus, you must like art if you know M. North—

although maybe you're just an art critic, but you don't seem the type. I have an eye for this stuff. Okay, so you have to come to one of my art classes. I teach mostly kids, but I have some adult classes too. Please say you'll come!"

I'd rather take a lighter to my art supplies than embarrass myself in an art class right now. What if I go and can't draw or paint anything and everyone sees what a failure I am? Or what if, by some miracle, I can paint, and she recognizes my art and realizes who I am? I'm not ready for that. And what would she think, knowing I stood here and lied to her face? But how do I say no to a potential new friend?

I don't know how long I'll be in Colorado or what the next few months hold for me, but I do know they might be easier to face if I have an ally in the art store owner.

I'm past the thirty minutes Charleigh gave me in the art store, but Dany was chatty, and after I agreed to attend at least one of her classes she walked me through the store giving recommendations for her favorite supplies. It's a small miracle I walked out without buying anything.

I loved Park's Deli, so my expectations are low for this new place, but to my surprise I'm immediately charmed. The exterior has been updated and it's quaint and welcoming. Park's was always a bit dirty and tired, but now the old blue awning is bright red with a block of cheese displayed right in the middle. The scratched, faded paint on the big front window is gone, making way for fresh gold letters that spell out the new name.

The updates don't stop on the outside either. Though the bell on the door and the coffee counter are the same, that's about all I recognize inside. All the booths with cracked leather seats are gone, replaced with small wood-top tables and modern black chairs. The walls aren't a dingy yellow beige anymore but a bright white, artsy photos of different types of cheese hanging all over them. The place is half-full, maybe even more packed than Park's would have been this time of year. I want to hate it, but it's so charming I can't. I don't see any cheese shop down here, though, and there's no sign of Charleigh, so I'll have to ask where it is.

I weave through the tables to the counter.

"Hey, how can I help you?" the friendly host asks.

"I'm looking for the cheese shop," I say, expecting them to tell me I'm in the wrong place despite all the cheese decor.

"Just up the stairs." They point to the back of the room, where a staircase sits just next to the kitchen doors.

"Thanks." I press my lips together in a tight smile and make my way over. Handmade rustic, chic-style signs dot the wall along the stairway, and I read each of them as I pass, smiling at how silly they are.

You Gouda Brie Kidding Me
Up to No Gouda
Gouda Vibes Only
To Brie or Not to Brie

At the top of the stairs is a small room with shelves to one side full of jams and crackers. There's a small table with two chairs, and the rest of the space is filled with a cheese display that puts

Whole Foods to shame. The glass enclosure is packed with wheels and blocks of cheese in various states of wholeness. Low-hanging light fixtures give the space a soft yellow glow. It's as cozy as any coffee shop I've been in, and I can't help but wonder if the same person who designed this space was in charge of the cheese puns on the stairs.

There's another person here browsing the shelves, but the space is small, and try as I might to give him space, there just isn't a lot up here. He seems like a local, dressed as he is in a flannel shirt with the sleeves rolled up, jeans, and hiking shoes.

"How 'bout those signs?" I gesture to the stairs. I'm not sure what compels me to speak up. Maybe the compact space has me feeling a little awkward or Dany's social energy rubbed off on me.

"Cheesy, huh?" He turns to me, eyes twinkling with his joke. His resemblance to Raymond Ablack is striking: floppy hair, a well-groomed beard, a smile that would make anyone's knees feel like jelly.

"Ha. I was half-expecting a 'Live, Laugh, Love' sign."

He chuckles, and I can't keep myself from smiling.

"Or maybe 'Live, Laugh, Limburger'? Or 'Live, Laugh, Lissome'?"

His joke is only funny to him since I don't recognize the words he uses, but I keep the smile plastered to my face. It's only polite.

"It sounds like you know your cheese. Is the stuff here any good?" I wander closer to the glass case, leaning in to inspect it. Small signs detail the names of the cheeses and give short descriptions of each.

"I like it," he says with a shrug and a grin. He examines a jar, turning it over in his hands.

I peek over my shoulder to see if maybe Charleigh's coming up the stairs, but no such luck. Do I have to keep this conversation going since I started it?

"How about the sandwiches downstairs? Any good? I don't know if you're local, but the place used to be called Park's Deli and it had this killer Rueben sandwich. The new owner has pretty big shoes to fill."

I try to read this guy's expressions. Should I leave him alone? He's had the same friendly smile on his face the whole time, and I can't tell if he's just being polite or enjoys socializing.

"You know, I'm hearing good things," he says, replacing the jar he was holding.

I nod, all out of things to say. My phone is in my back pocket, and just as I'm reaching for it to find out where the hell Charleigh is I hear footsteps coming up the stairs.

"Mara! I'm sorry I'm late." She catches her breath. Her hair is windblown and wild, and I reach to smooth down my own even though it's pulled into a long braid. "Oh, did you already meet Arjun?" She points between me and the stranger I've been chatting up.

How does she know his name?

And then I remember the owner's name is Arjun. My face, neck, and ears feel as if they're on fire. I'm not the praying type, but right now I'm begging whatever God is out there to do me the favor that this guy isn't looking at me.

"I, uh, did meet him," I say, enunciating each word. I sound so stupid right now, and it only compounds the urge to flee the building and never come back.

"Not formally, but she was just telling me an idea for a new sign in the hall there"—he gestures to the staircase—"and that she's eager to try the sandwiches downstairs." The grin on his face probably looks like a regular old friendly smile to Charleigh, but I see it for what it is: the kind of smile that holds an inside joke. "Anyway, it's nice to meet you, Mara."

He holds out a hand, and although I hope the building collapses and swallows me into it before I have to make eye contact with him, it doesn't. I shake his hand. His skin is softer than I imagined, his grip firm and steady. His eyes, his smile—they're full to the brim with humor, kindness. If I didn't just embarrass myself completely, I might find myself swooning a little.

Charleigh was right: he is easy on the eyes.

"The sandwiches are great. Isn't your chef someone you knew from culinary school days? I swear Ham told me that. Anyway, I just ordered our lunch." Charleigh turns to me. "But we can take it back to the cabin if you want—"

"Yes," I practically shout. Charleigh looks started. "Sorry, I'm just super tired. Big day."

"No problem," she says. Her voice has an edge of suspicion though as she turns to Arjun. "Any news on that car? We just got into town and I'm leaving in a couple days. Mara has no way of getting around."

"Still waiting to hear, but hoping my cousin texts me back soon. How long are you in town for?" he asks me.

"I'm not sure. At least a couple months."

"Mara just got out of a bad relationship, so she's—"

"Charleigh." I cut her off, glaring daggers.

"How are Ham and Alice?" Arjun asks, turning to my sister.

"Everyone is good. Ham says hi, and of course Alice does too."

They exchange smiles like old friends.

Downstairs, someone yells Charleigh's name and an order.

"I'll get that," I say, eager to leave. I almost trip over my own feet in my hurry to get to the staircase.

"It was nice to meet you, Mara!"

"Yeah, same." I wave my hand over my shoulder. "Charleigh?"

"I'll be right down."

I make a beeline for the front door, swearing never to set foot in this store again for as long as I'm in town.

3

$\mathscr{T}$he door to the Gouda Times Bistro closes behind me, and a mix of cold air and warm sun touches my cheeks. I relax for the first time all morning. This fresh mountain air is exactly what I need.

Charleigh breezes out behind me, tapping on her phone. "Good news—I secured a car for you."

"Oh, great," I say absently as she and I start the walk back to the car. She continues to talk, but I zone out, thinking of what an odd day it's turned out to be. On the one hand, I thoroughly embarrassed myself and I'm even more convinced I shouldn't have left my cabin today, but on the other, I met someone who loves my art and wants to be my friend.

My phone vibrates with a call, interrupting Charleigh and my thoughts.

"It's Jackie. I have to take this." I flash my screen at Charleigh, and she nods, gesturing that she's going to the car.

There's a bench on the sidewalk facing some of the stores, and I accept the call as I take a seat.

"Are you calling to beg me to come back to the east coast?

Miss me already?" I ask, tucking my free hand into my jacket pocket, my leg bouncing up and down.

Jackie and I got dinner the night before I moved out here, so it's been less than a week since we last saw each other.

"I might be. What could I bribe you with?"

An end to my creative block? Extracting the pieces of my brain still holding onto my last relationship?

"The price is too high even for you."

"There isn't anything I wouldn't do for my favorite client."

"You say all your clients are your favorite."

"How would you know that?"

"Because I was your first."

"Oh god, you really are my favorite."

Her deep laugh makes my mouth twitch with a smile. I have such a fondness for Jackie. She goes over and above as my agent, scheduling and attending all my meetings, doing any PR on my behalf—things she wouldn't have to do if I didn't paint under a pseudonym. We met as students at Pennsylvania State College. My senior project was a featured exhibition on campus. Jackie went to all the student exhibitions hoping to find her first clients so she could pursue her dream of becoming an art agent one day like her dad. She loves to tell people it was love at first painting, and it must have been, because she begged me to take a chance on her as an agent at the ripe old age of twenty-two. And here we are eight years later.

"You okay?" Jackie asks, hearing through my lame joke. "You sound a little off."

Jackie has always been more than just my agent. She's my friend too. Maybe one of my only friends considering how everything went down with Blair. Three years ago, when I lost my grandparents and things blew up with my sister, she started inviting me to her family's holiday dinners and rescheduled all my deadlines for two months. She gave me the space I needed to grieve, and I have no idea if another agent would have been so generous.

"I had the weirdest thing happen this morning. I saw one of my paintings in an art store and ended up having this whole conversation with the owner about me—without her knowing it was me, of course."

"You didn't tell her?"

"No. God, no."

"Why not?"

"I didn't know I was allowed to."

It's a lie, but it's easier than the truth right now. I could tell anyone I want to, but I'm scared. Jackie's about to call me out on it, so I brace myself.

"We agreed you get to decide who knows and who doesn't and when you're going to announce. Don't pawn this one off on me. Are you telling me you're still not ready to announce?"

"Would it help me financially? Like, in an immediate sense."

"It would potentially increase the value of the paintings you've already sold but wouldn't really make a difference until you're painting and selling again."

"Oh."

"So I'm guessing you're not interested."

"I couldn't tell one girl at an art store, much less the entire world. I don't think so."

The pseudonym wasn't even my idea to begin with. As soon as I agreed to let Jackie be my agent, I had a conversation with Ben about selling my art. We'd been together for four years—all of college—and he seemed really invested in my career. He was a business major and my very serious boyfriend, so bringing him in on the decision seemed like a good idea. He suggested a pseudonym, turning my words back on me: *"Painting is like putting pieces of my soul on the canvas, and by selling those things I'm selling my soul."* He said if I painted under a pseudonym I could see it as a business transaction, something that wasn't so personal.

At the time I thought this was profound, even romantic. It took a few months of therapy for me to realize Ben didn't actually care if I was selling my soul. I would have done anything he asked no matter the cost because I thought he loved me. Maybe he did love me, but he did that because he wanted to control me.

But the thought of revealing myself now feels like ripping off my clothes on TV. I'm not ready to be so exposed in such a public way. And doing so for financial reasons feels wrong.

"All right, well, whenever you're ready. I won't keep you, but I do have some news about the dinner I had with Everett Gerhardt last week."

"The German collector who owns the gallery in Paris? I hope he isn't looking for an exhibition. I told you before you went to that dinner I'm not agreeing to any exhibitions right now. I have no work to put in a gallery or sell."

"He actually owns galleries across Europe, and he *does* want an exhibition."

"I'm not—"

"Let me finish."

I roll my eyes. She's put on her agent voice, and this isn't a battle I'm going to pick.

"He wants to host an exhibition, but none of his galleries are available right now, so he found a space in Berlin to host you for a March exhibition. If it goes well, when his spaces open up in the summer your work will go up in all of them. He doesn't go out of his way like this for just anyone."

"All of them?"

"Which right now includes Paris, Amsterdam, and Frankfurt."

My heart races. This is huge. Despite the cut from the gallery, I've always preferred exhibitions to commissioned pieces. The freedom to paint what I want, the way a theme always comes together across a series of paintings. Commissions come with a lot more pressure. What if someone doesn't like what I made? It feels like a lot of money, and the risk of disappointment is too great.

Trying to wrap my mind around multiple exhibitions and what they'll do to my career is overwhelming. In the past five years, every exhibition has sold my pieces within three months. Commission offers have almost started to match the amount of money I make from selling out an exhibition, but four exhibitions before the year is even half-over? It's an opportunity any artist would be stupid to pass up.

But how can I say yes to this? I have no idea when I'll be painting again. If at all.

I hope Jackie said no to this guy the way I asked her to turn down everyone else, but I'm starting to suspect otherwise. My stomach clenches.

"Okay, well, did you tell him that I'm not—?"

"There's more. He wants a custom piece."

"Unfortunate for him since I—"

"He's offering two million for it."

My heart races, my jaw slackens, and there's a dropping sensation in my entire body as if I'm on the edge of a cliff with no railing. I've done well for myself over the years, but none of my pieces, no exhibition sales or commissions, have ever been worth over half a million dollars.

"I assume your silence is because you're as shocked as I was. Imagine my face at that dinner table."

"Did you tell him I'm not worth that much?" It comes out as a whisper, my voice deadly serious.

"What? Mara. No. You're absolutely worth that much."

"But you told him no, right?"

She doesn't say anything, and a chill overcomes me. The wind sounds like a train in my ears. Every car passing on the street sounds as if it's coming right for me. I want to be in my bed right now, hiding under my covers. Any other time, this conversation would be a dream come true, but this is becoming more and more like a nightmare. I have a feeling she's about to push me off the cliff.

"I told him yes."

I close my eyes, grateful that I'm sitting. *Deep breath in through the nose, out through the mouth . . .*

"Okay, but I'm not ready yet. I'm still not painting, Jackie. So I hope the next thing you're about to tell me is that he's flexible on dates and we'll call him when we're ready."

"I would love to tell you that, but he agreed to fully fund the exhibition if I was willing to commit. And I did."

"What kind of asshole asks for that kind of commitment without letting you go back to your artist first?"

"He probably thinks if you trust me enough to have your meetings, you trust me enough to make decisions without you. And if this were a year ago, you'd be trying to kiss me for agreeing to this."

My heart races a million miles per hour, my hands shake, and my stomach jumps into my throat. I hate that she's right and that I'll never have the words to explain to her why this is the worst possible thing to happen to me right now.

"What date did you lock in?" I manage to keep my voice even, but I know she can hear my anger.

"March fifteenth. You have six months."

"It's almost October, so I have five months."

"It's ten pieces for the exhibition and a custom, but he's flexible on the custom."

"Ten pieces?" My voice is louder than I intended it to be. I grip the edge of the bench until the pain in my hand is greater than the tight, twisty pain in my chest.

"I know you're not painting right now. Do you have any old pieces we never sold? Anything you can bring out from the vault, so to speak?"

I do, but I won't be using them for this. Those pieces are way too personal, and I swore never to show them to anyone when I painted them.

"No. Nothing."

"Okay." Jackie is undeterred by my negativity. "But this is why you went to Colorado, right? To get inspired. You're going to get unstuck soon, and you have five whole months to paint. I've seen you paint more in less time." Her voice is softer. She's the friend now, not the agent.

"It's different this time, Jackie."

A couple walk by me pushing a stroller, both holding lattes and looking lovesick at each other. They pause in front of me when their baby coos to snap a photo with their phone, preserving their perfect October afternoon.

The stark reality of my loneliness sets in as I watch the people around me. I lost my only friend—my partner of the last decade—my relationship with my sister is still a mess, and now my agent has thrown me under the bus.

"Why don't you believe you can do this?" she asks, and her voice is so tender my chin wobbles.

"This isn't just a case of self-doubt, Jackie. This is—it's . . ."

My inability to describe the problem succinctly has plagued me for months. It doesn't matter how I phrase it: "I lost my art," "I can't paint," or "my art left me"—none of it fully captures exactly what it is. It's packing for a trip but not being able to shake the feeling you've forgotten something. It's the craving for an apple that you're sure is in your pantry, but when you open the door it's empty, when just yesterday it was overflowing. It's trying to take a sip of your full glass of water and not getting even one drop. I've spent hours in therapy trying to come up with the right explanation, but each attempt falls flat. If I can't fully grasp it, how can I make Jackie understand?

"Whatever it is, it will pass. This is the opportunity of a lifetime. I don't want to put too fine a point on it, but this will make or break your career, Mara. Calling Everett Gerhardt to tell him we're backing out is not even on the table. If we lose this, we lose more than just this opportunity. Gerhardt is well-connected and not the type of person we want to piss off. So get to work and keep me updated."

Air doesn't seem to be getting all the way into my lungs. I close my eyes so the world will stop spinning. Jackie's right: I can't just ask her to call him and cancel if she signed a contract. Even if the man weren't well-connected, I can't keep refusing every opportunity that comes my way. Not only do I need the money, but people might stop calling if I consistently reject them. Getting around my creative block isn't just about finding myself again; it's about saving my career. I take a deep, controlled breath to fight the pounding of my pulse in my ears.

"I have to go, Jackie. I'll call you later." I end the call and power walk to the car like maybe I can outpace my panic.

Did I really spend the past six months believing this moment wouldn't come? That I wouldn't eventually be faced with the reality that losing my art doesn't just mean losing my identity but also the thing I've spent my whole life working toward? Did I really believe I could hold onto my career without being able to paint?

The answer to all that is yes. I believed those things with the naivety of a woman who took her career—her creativity—for granted. But I swear if I get it back, if the day comes when I can paint again, I'll never let anything or anyone take it away.

4

"Did you miss me already?" I say to Charleigh, who calls minutes after pulling out of the driveway to head home. She was here for a week, and as grateful as I am for everything she did for me, I couldn't help but breathe a sigh of relief when I walked back into the cabin after saying goodbye.

"Actually, I think I left a pair of shoes in the bedroom. Would you mind checking really fast?"

"I can just mail them to you."

"Could you just check, please? I'd rather not spend the next day and a half wondering."

I roll my eyes, glad she can't see me, and shuffle to the guest bedroom clutching my warm coffee mug. The sun is just barely coming up and I'm not fully awake yet. Charleigh left at an obscene hour, but it felt rude not to say goodbye. She made freezer meals and scrubbed the cabin so hard the dust has sworn never to return—the least I could do was wake up early to hug her. It was awkward, but it left me with hope. Hope that maybe the bridge I burned isn't beyond repair.

"There're no shoes in here," I say, glancing around the room.

"Check the closet?"

Wedging the phone between my shoulder and ear, I open the closet door, revealing a large plastic bag. I peek inside it, but instead of shoes I find a heap of art supplies: brushes, canvases of varying sizes, and tubes of paint.

"What the hell, Charleigh?"

"I thought you might need more supplies after the driveway incident. The girl at the store helped me pick everything out. Hopefully, this replaces everything you need." She sounds so pleased with herself. Her smile oozes through the phone.

I clench my jaw so hard it hurts my teeth. This is so like Charleigh, thinking she knows what's best for people and butting in where she's not wanted. "I broke my brushes for a reason," I say, closing the closet door with my foot and leaving the supplies where they are. I sit on the edge of the bed clutching my mug, hugging it against my body.

"You're not painting right now, I know, but you will be soon. You've had creative lulls before, and when this one is over, you'll need supplies."

Yet another person who doesn't understand. My insides curl up and all the fight leaves me.

When I don't say anything Charleigh sighs. "Don't forget Arjun is coming by with the car later," she says, not hiding her annoyance. She clearly wants me to fight it out, but that's not my style.

"Drive safe." My voice is a whisper, and I hang up, tossing my phone on the bed. I take a big gulp of coffee. It's too hot for my mouth, but I welcome the heat. The pain is a distraction from my frustration.

Why does no one believe how bad things are? Sure, I've gone

the occasional month or so with no ideas or paintings, but it's been *six months*. Either everyone knows something I don't or they're determined to misunderstand me. No matter how many times I say I can't paint, all I get back is "it's just a matter of time."

But I don't have time anymore. My agent's signed me up for an exhibition in five months, and I have nothing to show for it. If I don't get started soon my career is over.

So if it won't come to me, then I'll just have to take it.

I haul the supplies into the sunroom, taking out the canvases and dumping the paints and brushes unceremoniously onto the floor. Without an easel, I prop the canvas against the couch so I don't have to hunch over it. I choose a tube of paint at random, feeling its weight, demanding inspiration. But nothing comes. I squeeze a large dot of paint onto the canvas and let it sit there. Staring at it, I wait for the pictures that always come to me, wait for the whispers of creativity to guide me, wait for my fingers to itch. But still nothing comes.

A surge of frustration spurs me to slash my brush across the canvas, through the dot of paint. A dark red streak appears across the snow-white, but it does nothing to satisfy the urgency growing inside me that I need to paint, and I need to paint now.

With forceful strokes I push the dark red paint around, filling the canvas. I shrug off my cardigan, warm even though there's no fire going in the room. The bristles bend at weird angles—I'm ruining the brush and I don't care. A rush of power sweeps through me, and my limbs buzz. I change my grip, crushing the very expensive brush against the canvas. When I run out of paint I add more. When the brush is destroyed, I grab another.

I wreck eight brushes before I'm spent. They lie where they landed after I threw them, the canvas covered in childish scribbles. I feel hollowed-out, as if someone took a spoon to my soul and scraped the edges raw.

Drawing my legs to my chest, I hold them there. I press my forehead to my knees and let my flannel pajama pants absorb my tears.

I wanted Jackie and Charleigh to be right. I wanted to just believe I could paint and be able to, but it doesn't work like that. And they will never understand.

I don't know how long I sit on the couch taking in the damage I've done. It was an expensive temper tantrum, and Charleigh would probably scream if she knew I destroyed most of the brushes she bought me. I'm torn between a desire to clean up my mess and the idea of keeping it on display as some kind of sick reminder I can't force my creativity. But a knock on the door keeps me from deciding.

Who's that?

Charleigh's voice pops into my head from this morning: *Don't forget Arjun is coming by with the car.*

"Shit." I scramble off the floor of the sunroom and take inventory of my outfit. I still haven't changed out of my flannel pajamas and my hands are covered in paint. There's probably paint on my face, and I don't even want to think about what my hair looks like. Do I let him see me like this?

Another set of knocks and a voice come through the door. "Mara?"

Butterflies go off in my stomach. *Oh god, I've been crying. Do I even want to know what I look like right now?* I open the camera on my phone and put it in selfie mode. Exactly what I thought: my face is splotchy and my eyes are red-rimmed. My hair is in a messy bun, but not the cute kind.

"Um, be there in just a second," I yell through the door and bolt to the bedroom, throwing on the jeans and plaid top lying on my floor. Yanking out my hair tie, I finger-comb my long hair, hoping my look is more "messy chic" and not "worried-for-you messy."

When I open the front door, I know my face is flushed, and I try to conceal my slightly labored breathing with a big smile and slow, deep breaths.

"You got the memo," Arjun says, a bright smile lighting up his whole face.

"About the car? Yeah, my sister—"

"No, about the plaid." He points to my shirt, a blue plaid, and then to his, a blue-green plaid.

"Oh." The corners of my lips twitch. "I guess I did."

Arjun tosses a set of keys up into the air and catches them. There's an easy playfulness about him that strikes a chord of envy in me. "Want to check out the car?"

"Um, yes. Let me get my shoes."

I close the door and lean against it, squeezing my eyes closed. I was not prepared for this. I desperately want to crawl into bed and hide under the covers until tomorrow, but I need a car, and this probably won't take long. *You can do this, Mara.* I stuff my feet into the closest pair of shoes and run my fingers through my hair one more time.

In my driveway is a bright blue Honda CRV. Arjun waits for me by the driver's side door, and the stomach butterflies come back. I can't tell if I'm nervous about socializing or if being around such a cute guy is having an effect on me.

Birds and bugs chirp and squeak around us, and though the

midday sun is warm, a cool breeze whips my hair in front of my face as the gravel crunches beneath my feet. I tuck my hair behind my ears and let the beauty of this small moment settle deep in my bones.

"Here she is." He holds his arms out as if I just won the car on *The Price Is Right*.

"She's beautiful." The edges of my lips tug into a smile.

He holds out the keys to me. "Should we take her for a spin?"

My lips part, but no sound comes out. Arjun must sense my discomfort.

"Or maybe just a ride home," he suggests, his tone light and easy.

"Sure," I say with a nod.

Our fingertips brush as I take the keys from him, sending an unexpected jolt of electricity through me. *Is this what happens to me when I haven't been touched by a man in six months? Jesus.*

The door squeaks as Arjun opens it for me, and I climb in. The car smells earthy—hints of wine and cheese, sweat and deodorant—but also like old leather and dust, like a car that hasn't been used in a while. Arjun shuts the door and taps on the window, leaning on the side of the car. I adjust the seat, getting acquainted with it. When I crank the handle on the doorframe the glass pane lowers between us. He's standing so close I can see the exact color of his irises. I thought they were the same color as his pupils, but I can see now the various shades of brown. It reminds me of strong tea, the way it looks black until you catch it in just the right light.

"What do you think?" he asks.

"I haven't seen manual windows in ages," I say.

"Just wait till you see the cassette player. I've got one of those special cassettes that lets you hook up your phone."

"Well, this car is a modern marvel."

"My Grannie certainly thought so."

"This belongs to your grandmother?"

"Belonged. Past tense."

"Oh no. I'm so sorry." I cover my mouth with my hands.

"For what?" He seems genuinely confused.

"Your grandmother . . . you said past tense."

He chuckles. "I can see how that was confusing. Grannie isn't dead—we just revoked her car privileges. She's a danger to all drivers everywhere."

A laugh bubbles up from my belly, escaping before I have a chance to contain it. "How old is she?" I ask.

"Somewhere between eighty-five and one hundred and five."

"Over a hundred years old? Really?"

Arjun grins. "It's possible. Grannie's sister lived to be 107. The women in my family tend to live forever. But Grannie either can't remember how old she is and won't admit to it or doesn't want to tell us."

"Sounds like my grandmother." I smile.

"How old is she?"

"She died. A few years back."

"I'm so sorry." His voice softens.

"Thank you. I miss her. Well, I miss both my grandparents a lot." I stare at the cabin wistfully. "This was theirs."

"Did they leave it to you?" he asks. It doesn't feel like he's being nosy or just polite; he asks like he's genuinely curious about the answer.

"My sister and me. They knew we loved it, and my parents have no use for it."

"Do you like living here?"

"I've only been here for a week, but so far so good," I say with a polite smile. It's not the most authentic answer, but I've already embarrassed myself in front of this guy once—no need to spill my guts to him as well.

"Well, hey, how 'bout that ride home?" he says and walks around to the passenger side of the car.

"Where do you live?" I clear my throat and start the engine.

"Green door cabin just that way." He points down the road. "I'm your neighbor."

"I thought an old man lived there."

"He does. It's me. I'm actually seventy-five."

"You look so good for your age. You have to tell me your secrets."

"It's the cheese."

"And here I've been hydrating and moisturizing like a fool."

Arjun laughs a real full-bodied laugh, and the butterflies float to my chest.

It's a short drive, less than five minutes. I try to focus on the road, but I can't help myself, and the whole drive over I sneak glances at him. In snippets, I notice the way his hand rests on his thigh and the slope of his shoulders. It's been a long time since I felt the stir of new attraction. Where Ben was all bulk and ex-football player arms, Arjun is attractive in the boy-next-door kind of way.

I shift in my seat and grip the wheel a little tighter.

When I veer onto the gravel patch that serves as his driveway and cut the engine, I turn to him and ask, "How long have you lived here?" with a nod to his cabin.

"Bought it about four years ago."

"When I was a kid, there was an old man who lived here, and he was really grumpy and kinda mean. There's actually a trail behind all the cabins up here, and Charleigh and I would walk it as kids. We'd always tiptoe when we passed his cabin, holding our breath, thinking if he found us we'd end up like some fairy-tale kids."

Arjun and I share a chuckle at my memory, and for a moment I relax into the easiness of our conversation. It reminds me of the early days with Ben, the way we connected so quickly. How we fell into each other's lives so easily and still crashed and burned. The memories of him start to crowd the small space, and I stiffen, leaning a little farther away from Arjun.

"Would you like to come in? I just made lunch."

When I look at Arjun I catch him studying me, his brow furrowed a little and his gaze fixed on mine. *Did he notice me shift away?*

"That's really kind of you, but I've got to . . . get back." I look down at my hands.

"No problem. Would you mind waiting here for just a minute though?"

Before I can say yes or no, he's out of the car and sprinting up his front steps into the house. He emerges less than a minute later holding a glass food container, then he comes around to the driver's side window and hands it through to me.

"You didn't have to do that."

"'No one leaves empty-handed if there's hot food in my house.' Something my Grannie always says. I live by it too." His smile gets warmer every time I look at him, the same way the sun gets warmer as it rises in the sky.

Whatever's inside is steaming up the glass container. It looks like rice topped with some kind of yellow sauce. I crack the lid and inhale. Cinnamon, turmeric, clove, and chili. My stomach grumbles.

"Oh my god. This smells amazing. What is it?"

"A Ghosh family classic. Chana dal. It's got lentils and chick-peas and a spice blend that I can't legally share with you because my mother would sue me if she knew I were handing out her secrets."

I replace the lid, blinking rapidly. Something about the warm dish in my hand and the kindness of a near stranger has opened the floodgates inside me, and once again I have to refrain from crying in front of Arjun.

"Wow. Thank you for this. And again for the car." I set down the Tupperware and start the car, ready to book it out of here. "Oh! Wait. My sister didn't tell me how much I owe you for the car."

"Nothing."

"What do you mean?" I ask.

Arjun hesitates, biting his lower lip. The action makes my stomach drop, but I push it away. It still feels weird to think about being single, much less letting myself be attracted to whomever.

"Your sister paid for it. But you didn't hear that from me!"

"That's some older sister shit," I mumble.

Arjun makes a noise halfway between a snort and a laugh. An awkward silence fills the space between us.

"Let me know if you need anything else," he says, tapping the side of the car twice and stepping back.

I nod and swallow hard, backing out of the driveway. He holds up his hand to say goodbye. Even as I drive away, checking my rearview mirror, he's still standing in the same spot watching me as I go.

5

I'm halfway out my front door digging around my purse for my keys as the strap slides down my shoulder, squeezing Arjun's empty glass container between my arm and side and trying not to trip over my untied boot lace when my phone rings.

"You will just have to wait," I say to whoever's calling, yanking the door closed and hoping as I lock it that I don't drop anything. I've already spilled coffee on my jeans, stubbed my toe on the couch corner, and burned my finger while making eggs. I'm starting to think I should have just stayed in bed. But I've done that every day for the past week. I'm overdue a trip out of the house.

Door locked, I manage to slip my phone out of my pocket while it's still ringing, but it practically throws itself out of my hand and onto my porch facedown. The vibrating stops. I've missed the call.

"Oh, fuck you," I curse at the phone before scooping it up. As I lean over my purse strap slips down to my forearm. A half-scream leaves my mouth, and with more force than necessary I sling the purse strap around my neck to wear it across my body instead.

I turn the phone over and relax when I see the screen is crack-free. The missed call is from Charleigh, and I tense, huffing out a breath. The cold air billows in a white cloud from my mouth. We haven't talked since she surprised me with those supplies the day she left. I needed some space. That's just like her to buy me supplies and the car without talking to me about it first.

On the one hand, I'm grateful. I really don't have the kind of money I used to. But on the other, it makes me feel like a child again.

I get settled in the car, blowing on my gloved hands while I wait for it to heat up and taking a few centering breaths. It's only October, but it already cold out in the mornings. By the time the car is warm, I feel a little more ready to face the day. And Charleigh.

"Hi. Sorry I missed your call," I say when she picks up. "I was dropping everything I've ever owned."

"That's fine," she says with a small, forced laugh. "I was just checking in. Wanted to make sure you got the car and that it's working out for you."

I've had the car for almost a week, but I haven't taken it anywhere before today. I've only left the house to go on a few hikes by the cabin. I was hoping they'd inspire me, but so far they've only helped me fall asleep at night. An improvement, but not the one I was hoping for.

"The car is fine." I pause. "You didn't have to pay for it."

"I know, but you're not really working right now, and—"

"I'm grateful, okay? But I'm not a starving artist or anything." I press the speakerphone button and stick my phone in a cupholder before backing out of the driveway. I sound petulant, but I hate when she thinks she knows best and does stuff like this without me asking. More than once in my early years as an artist she sent a gift card for my favorite Indian restaurant with enough money for me to get takeout for an entire month.

"Look, I wasn't trying to— Why won't you just let me take care of you?" I hear the edge in her voice and can almost see her rubbing her temples, pinching her lips together so they disappear into a line.

"Because I don't need to be taken care of." I think of the dishes piled up in the sink, my clothes strewn across the cabin, and the dust bunnies that have already started to collect in the corners of the house. She knows I'm lying, but she's going to let me, because this is what we do.

When we were younger, our favorite game to play was Pretend. She'd be a doctor and I'd be her patient. I'd be a princess and she'd be a knight. We never stopped playing, really. The game just changed.

Charleigh sighs, probably exhausted by me, and the sound feels like being stabbed. I open my mouth to make my excuses and get off the phone, but she starts to talk again. "Well, hey, I won't keep you, but I wanted to talk about Thanksgiving." She drags out the last word as if trying to soften the blow, but it still hits hard, paralyzing me.

I've ignored Thanksgiving for the past two years. Ben even tried to convince me to go eat with him and his family once or twice, but I always refused. I plan to spend this Thanksgiving the way I've spent the past two: alone.

"I know it's early, but we usually come up to the cabin, and we wanted some time to make plans if you didn't want to, ya know. We don't have to—"

"Uh, Charleigh." I cut her off. There's a siren screaming in my brain, warning the rest of my body: panic! Panic now! I clench the steering wheel and try to fight the sensation of dread spreading through me. I guide the car to the shoulder. "Sorry, I—I'm driving into town and I'm about to go through that dead spot. I'll text you."

"Yeah, okay. Text whenever," Charleigh says as I end the call with a shaking hand.

I rest my forehead against the steering wheel, squeezing my eyes shut, holding my entire body taut, trying to stop the quaking.

My grandmother was very sick before she died three years ago. Her death came slowly and we all got to say our goodbyes. My grandfather's death three days later was unexpected, surprising us all until we learned he died of heart failure. He loved Grammy and he didn't want to be without her. They both died the week before Thanksgiving, which was their favorite holiday. So the day after the funeral we gathered for a meal, determined to honor these people we loved so much. It was a small dinner—just me, Charleigh and her family, and our parents. It went as well as could be expected.

And then everything went to shit.

I thought that week couldn't get worse after losing my grand-parents one right after the other, but after that dinner I didn't speak to Charleigh for three years. And I no longer participate in Thanksgiving.

A few deep breaths later, I'm on the road again. Just thinking about the Thanksgiving from hell three years ago is enough to send me into a spiral, which is why I don't participate in the holiday any longer. Maybe one year soon I'll be able to, but this is not that year.

By the time I park I've already composed a text to Charleigh in my head. I type it out and send it before I can chicken out.

Can we skip Thanksgiving? Do Christmas, maybe?

Sounds good. *thumbs-up emoji*

The guilt gnaws at me. I tap my thumbs against the sides of the phone. This dance we're doing is discouraging. Two steps forward, three steps back.

Sorry. And hey, thank you for the car.

You're welcome. <3

My sister's trying to rebuild the burned bridge between us, and I keep setting fire to it all over again. I stare at our text conversation. At the heart emoji Charleigh sent.

At least only one of us is an arsonist.

* * *

I don't want to walk into the bistro right during lunch hour, so I slip into The Artist's Outlet to kill some time. The store looks empty. It was this empty the last time I was here too. I double-check the hours on the door to make sure it's actually open. It is, and the combination of soft K-pop and the vague scent of new pencils and fresh canvas transports me to a calmer place. The tension of this morning slides off my shoulders.

I end up in the aisle with the oil paints, scanning the tubes for a color that might spark an idea, but no inspiration comes. I'm starting to think maybe I came here for the same reason other girls check their exes' social media: mourning, wondering about the possibilities, self-loathing.

The faint sound of someone singing along with the music floats to me from farther into the store, and I follow it. Dany's propped against the arm of a chair in front of the fireplace, facing away from me, her legs draped over the other arm. There's a sketch pad on her lap and a charcoal pencil in her hand. Her short blonde hair sways as she moves her head back and forth with the music. In her sketchbook I see a drawing, and for the briefest second my fingers itch. I flex and clench them, but the familiar ache is gone almost as fast as it appeared.

"What are you working on?" I ask, trying not to startle her. I'm unsuccessful, though, and Dany yelps.

She twists around in the chair, a hand pressed to her chest, and as the shock wears off her face lights up with a big smile. "Mara, right? Hey! How are you? Can I help you with anything?"

"Yes, Mara. You remembered." This makes me smile. I love when people remember my name. Maybe because I've spent my entire career nameless. "I was in the area and I can't help myself when it comes to art supplies."

"Oh my god, I totally understand. Anything catch your eye?"

"Just whatever you've got there." I point to her sketch pad.

Her smile takes on a shy quality, but she stands, bringing her work to me.

I take the sketchbook and admire her near-perfect rendering of the fireplace. "Dany, this is . . . this is really good." She's captured the shadows and bumps of every stone. Her technique is flawless, but more than that, she's captured the coziness and warmth a fireplace brings to a room. I glance up from the sketch pad so she can see the sincerity on my face.

She fiddles with the ends of her hair, leaving little black streaks in the bright blonde from the charcoal on her fingers. "It's just a little doodle," she says with all the modesty of a girl who's never been complimented on her work.

I flip through the sketchbook expecting to see maybe a couple of drawings, but nearly every page is full of faces, trees, gardens, mountains, Main Street storefronts, or random objects from the store. They're drawn with charcoal or colored pencils or fountain pens, all beautiful, truthful sketches that make me long for an empty sketchbook and pencil.

"You're really talented. Thanks for sharing these with me. Did you study art in college?"

She gets a sad look on her face. "Sort of. What about you?"

"Yep."

"Ahh, this is so great. I have no art friends, just a bunch of students. What do you do now?"

"Still an artist." I give Dany a pained smile and hand her back her sketchbook. "Is drawing what you do most?" *Time to steer this conversation away from me . . .*

"Yes! Well, I kind of do everything. Jack of all trades, master of none and all that. But I definitely prefer drawing to painting or sculpting. I paint too and teach that, but I do prefer drawing. I love watercolor in particular, but I never finish anything I start when I use watercolor—I don't know why. What about you? What do you use?"

"I haven't used anything but oils for years. I can't even remember the last time I sketched or drew anything."

"Oh my gosh, well, I just got these pencils in. I'd love for you to test them." She shoves the pencil from her hand into mine and practically launches herself into the aisles. She scurries back with a fresh sketch pad, pencil sharpener, and eraser and ushers me over to one of the chairs in front of the fireplace.

"Right now?" I ask as I sit, items transitioning from her to me.

"Oh gosh, I didn't even think— Are you busy? You can totally take that stuff home with you. Or you can try it here and then take it home with you and it's on the house. From one artist to another," she says with a wink.

I freeze, unable to form words. I have to remind myself she doesn't know who I am. *Why don't I just tell her? Can I? Should I?* I've spent the past decade in a bubble with Ben, not making new friends, attending my own exhibitions as a ghost, letting Jackie talk about my career for me. I've never had to think about revealing my identity because I haven't let anyone new into my life in years. I had Ben and my best friend Blair and I didn't need anyone else. But my world is opening up now, and I have no idea how to navigate it.

"No," I say, still composing myself. "No, I have time. I just need to drop off something at the bistro, but I wanted to avoid the lunch hour." I settle back into the chair, opening the new sketchbook. I twirl the pencil in my fingers and try to lose myself in the blank page.

The problem is I've always hated the white, empty space on a page or canvas. It's the colors I love, mixing and experimenting until I find the exact right shade that fits whatever I've got in mind. But my mind has been empty of color for months now.

I tap the pencil against the page. Dany settles back into her chair, legs draped over the edge, losing herself in her drawing again.

"What inspires you, Dany? What do you do when you're stuck?"

She looks thoughtful for a moment. "Everything inspires me. How can I get stuck when I just have to look outside and the whole world is waiting to be drawn? Every minute of every day the shadows are different than they were just a minute ago." She gestures toward the windows at the front of the store where the light streams in. "I just love trying to capture the way something was for a moment in time. Because it's gone before you can blink, but I've got it on the page. And it was real and it was there for one moment, and I have proof." She holds up her sketchbook, displaying the fireplace drawing.

"Yeah, that's . . ." I say, staring again at my blank page. I understand what she's describing, but it feels out of reach.

"Are you stuck?"

"I've been stuck for a while." I set the sketch pad on the small table between our chairs. "I think I'll just . . ."

"Wait." Dany's arm shoots out. "Let's—can we try something?" Her hand rests on my arm, heavy.

I wince. "I don't know. I really—"

"I promise if it doesn't work, I'll—well, I don't know what I'll do, but you can vow never to trust the crazy lady at the art store again."

This makes me laugh, breaking the spell of uncertainty. I sit back down, taking a chance on this girl.

Dany scoots to the edge of her chair, leaning toward me. "Draw a vertical line on the right side of the page," she instructs, gesturing to my book.

Before starting, I use the pencil sharpener, prepping my tool. I press the tip of the pencil against the paper and it glides down the page, smooth and satisfying. Tiny droplets of charcoal spill from the line I've drawn.

"Now draw another, parallel, on the opposite side of the page."

I do this as well, the scent of the charcoal filling my nose. It takes me back to art class, elementary school, the first time I drew with a cheaper version of this pencil. I went home and begged my parents to buy me a set, and to my delight they took me to an art supplies store that night to purchase "fancy pencils," as my mom liked to call them, and a new sketchbook. Warmth spreads through me at the memory.

"Now connect those two lines with a horizontal line at the top."

I connect the two lines and wait for more instruction.

"Yep, perfect," Dany says. "Now draw a smaller version of that shape inside the shape, but sort of in the middle and toward the bottom." She gestures to the page, tracing the lines I should draw with her finger.

I do this and show her. "Like this?" I ask.

She nods, a smile breaking across her face. "Yes! Now look—you've drawn the fireplace!"

"I see what you did there." I narrow my eyes at her, smirking. I glance between my lines and the actual fireplace, and she's right: my lines are the shape of a fireplace.

"Sometimes getting started is all it takes to get unstuck," Dany says and reclines back in her chair, a pleased look on her face. She dips her head back to her own drawing, and I do the same.

As I stare at my lines and back at the actual structure, a ghost of a picture starts to take shape on the page, and I see exactly what needs to be drawn. It comes easier than I expect, bringing the shadows and shape of the stones to life with my pencil.

Maybe because Dany got me started and a little bit of momentum goes a long way.

After some time—though I don't know how much—Dany taps on my page with the end of her pencil. I blink, clearing my eyes. I must have totally zoned out.

"Can I see?" she asks.

I hand her the sketchbook and dig my phone out of my purse to check the time. An hour gone, though I could have sworn it was years.

"Mara! Amazing! See? Not so stuck." This time her smile is paired with pride, and when she hands the sketchbook back to me I let myself be celebrated for this small thing.

I study what I've sketched. There's nothing remarkable about it, though I can admire my own basic drawing technique. It isn't much in the way of my career and prepping for an exhibition, but it's something.

It's proof I'm still here.

6

The bistro's nearly empty when I walk in. The smell of fresh bread and coffee lingers in the air and my stomach grumbles, reminding me I skipped lunch. There's no sign of Arjun on this level, so I make my way upstairs, but he isn't there either. My sigh is a mix of relief and disappointment. As much as I enjoyed our brief encounter last week, spending more time with someone as attractive as him could be a distraction. I need to be figuring out how to paint again, not flirting with the cheese shop guy.

I'll just have to leave the container on the table here, but I should at least leave a note to say thank you.

I set the container on the little table and rummage through my purse for something to leave a note. I have nothing, and the register up here is just a tablet. I jog back downstairs, bringing the container with me. There's no one around at all, so I go behind the counter, finding a pen and scrap paper at the register. I scribble a quick note and add a doodle of a girl eating and looking happy then return the pen to its place and chuckle at my little picture. I should send it to Jackie, but she probably wouldn't find it very funny.

"Hello, stranger." The doorbell jingles as Arjun walks through the door carrying a large container.

I freeze. I'm still standing behind the counter. I crumple up the note in my hand and hide it behind my back.

Wine bottles clang together as Arjun moves closer to the counter, his biceps straining against the fabric of his navy Henley. He tosses his hair out of his eyes and flashes me a thousand-watt smile.

My mouth goes dry. "Hey." I drag out the word, trying to give my brain time to catch up.

"You looking for a job?" His smile becomes a smirk as he sets the box on one of the barstools. His chest rises and falls as he catches his breath, leaning on the box.

"Yes. No. I'm—nope—this isn't—"

He raises his eyebrows. "Isn't . . . what? Am I being robbed?"

"Oh my god, I'm not stealing. That's—"

"I'm kidding," he says, and I swear his eyes twinkle.

"Oh." My shoulders drop from my ears and my chest loosens. "Ha. Right. Sorry."

"Can I help you with something though?"

"I actually just stopped by to return the Tupperware." I gesture to the food container next to the register. "I just came down to write a little thank-you note."

He reaches for the container, examining it. "That was nice of you. Where's the note?"

"Oh, it was . . . just a . . ." I wave one of my hands, trying to dismiss it, but then I realize how silly I must look with one hand still behind my back.

"Is the note what you're hiding?" He smirks again, and damn it if it isn't an adorable smirk.

"No," I say exactly the way a guilty person would say it, and Arjun raises his eyebrows at me again. I bring both my hands around and open them, the crumpled note revealing itself. My cheeks heat.

He plucks the note out of my hand and opens it. His eyes are bright as he studies the doodle.

"I know it's stupid," I say.

"This isn't stupid at all. It's adorable," he says, and warmth floods me.

"Okay, well, I think I'll get going." I walk out from behind the counter. "And I'll just take that . . ." I reach for the note in his hand, but he snaps his hand closed and moves his arm back in one swift motion. I lose my balance with the momentum and reach out to brace myself, but my hands land squarely on Arjun's chest.

He grabs my arms, steadying me. I catch a hint of woodsmoke and the cold air he brought inside with him, but I'm also close enough now to smell a hint of wine on his breath. "Sorry, I'm keeping this one," he says, his voice soft.

I clear my throat and take a step back, tugging at the hem of my jacket and adjusting my beanie. Arjun tucks my doodle into his pocket. I lean into the awkwardness as I walk past him and head to the door.

"Joke's on you—that's not even my best work. So I'm going to go home and work on . . . more of that . . ." I somehow end up doing finger guns and quickly tuck my hands into my jacket pockets when I realize how dumb I look.

"Hey, actually, if you don't have anything going on, I just got back from a local vineyard and have some product to test out."

Arjun hoists the box of wine off the barstool and angles his body toward the stairs. "Care for a drink?"

"I ... um ..."

All that awaits me after this is the silence of my cabin and the taunting of my paintbrushes. I don't have much to go back to, but the siren call of alone time is tempting. Though so is a glass of wine with a handsome cheesemonger ...

"Just one drink?" he asks as if I've already said no and he's promising me it'll be worthwhile. He asks with hope, the kind young men have when they're asking a beautiful girl to dance. It's the kind of question I haven't been asked in a long time.

"Okay, sure. Just one though," I say with a tone of authority, trying to convince myself more than anything.

He leads me upstairs and sets the box on the floor by the table, gesturing for me to sit. When I do he disappears into the kitchen.

I take off my coat and drape it over the back of the chair. I haven't had drinks with a man who isn't Ben in years. I tried hanging out with my guy friends in college a few times after we graduated, but Ben didn't like it. Eventually, I just stopped hanging out with any guys but Ben. And then eventually I stopped hanging out with anyone at all who wasn't Ben or Blair. At the time I believed they were all I needed and I didn't really mind. It took a few weeks of therapy to realize he'd been closing in my social circle to maintain control over me.

But now my stomach flutters. Arjun is funny and cute, and it feels weird to be on a non-date in a cheese shop. At least I hope he doesn't think it's a date.

When Arjun reappears he's got two wineglasses in one hand and a small wooden cutting board with cheese on it in the other, and I've got anxiety over this whole thing. "I hope you like cheese," he says.

"What kind of person doesn't like cheese?" I sound way more confident than I feel. *I hope he opens the wine soon.*

"I don't know, but I don't trust any of them," he says, deadpan. I like his humor.

I reach for a slice of thick light orange cheese before he's even set the board on the table.

"That's an aged cheddar I got from a farm a couple hours from here. Seven Stars Farm. They're my oldest supplier."

The cheese is nutty and sharp, and it crumbles as I bite into it. I let the crumbs fall onto my shirt, brushing them off. Maybe I should care more, but this cheese is sending me into another universe.

"I think I just met God."

"This wine will go really nicely with that," Arjun says with laughter in his voice. He holds the black bottle by its neck. An elegant white number seven is printed on the black label, but I only notice it briefly before he opens the bottle. A few swift twists of the opener and one sharp, smooth pull and the cork is free, completely intact. *Was that sexy, or am I lonely?* He screws the cork off the opener and sniffs the purple-stained end. "Black cherry and . . ." He holds it out to me.

I lean in and sniff. "Cork?" I suggest.

He smiles and touches the cork to his nose again. "Toast."

"Toast?"

"From the oak barrels."

He pours a small amount of the wine into one glass, then he holds it up, swirling the liquid around. He brings it to his nose and inhales before finally taking a small sip. "Tastes like . . ." He pauses to take another sip.

"Black cherry? Toast?"

"Red wine." He gives me a wolfish grin, and a small laugh escapes me.

When he hands me the glass he just drank out of, I hesitate before taking it. Sharing a glass is an intimate act by any standard. Do I ask for my own? I don't want to be weird, so I take it and try to turn the glass away from where his lips were for a small sip.

"So you're not a wine connoisseur?"

"I may have just repeated all the information they gave me at the vineyard."

"Ahh. So you were trying to impress me?" I drain my glass and slide it across the table for a refill.

"Were you impressed?"

"I was. For, like, thirty seconds."

"Then mission accomplished." He pours a more generous amount of wine this time.

I accept the glass and try to hide my smile with it as I take a big drink of the wine. This is so much better than spending the evening by myself in my cabin. Where my cabin is cold and empty, Arjun's presence is warm and full. He opens a second bottle of wine, the same swift, professional movements stirring up a very unprofessional feeling in my body. Something I was not prepared to feel today even if I have been single for six months.

"Your sister told me you're an artist." Arjun pours the white wine from the freshly opened bottle into the empty glass on the table but doesn't drink it yet. He sets the bottle down, also black with a black label, this one with a white number six, then leans on the table holding his elbows with his hands, the woodsmoke from him mingling with the alcohol from the wine and salt from the cheese. It's a smell I want to put on a canvas.

I lean in too, resting my arms on the table but still clutching my wineglass, making the small gap between us even smaller. "I am an artist," I say, twirling the wineglass in my fingers, unsure how much Charleigh told him. Unsure how much I should say. "I paint. Well, I used to." I eat another piece of cheese and follow it with a gulp of my drink. The wine mingles with my blood, loosening my muscles, warming me. My face feels hot and my shoulders relax as if the wine has grown hands and pushed them away from my ears.

"What do you do now instead of painting?"

"Nothing, actually. I'm just . . . in between projects." It's not a lie, but it's also not entirely the truth.

"Tell me, what does the life of an artist between projects look like?"

I both love and hate that he's digging for more. I appreciate a man who likes to dig a little deeper, who isn't satisfied with just surface-level, but I'm not sure I'm ready to hand over a shovel just yet. "I sit around in cheese shops drinking wine with handsome strangers."

This comment elicits a full smile from him—one that shows off a set of white teeth made by God or orthodontics. It's a gorgeous smile, and I adjust in my seat. His smile is doing things to my body, sending signals I haven't felt in a long time.

"I'm hardly a stranger now, right? We must've moved into acquaintance territory. I've fed you twice now." He nods to the cheese board, not even half-empty.

Small crumbs of cheese cling to the wood. The orange-white bright against the dark wood reminds me of stars in the night sky, flecks of paint in my dark hair.

"The only things I know about you," I say, "are your name, a few family details, where you live, and that you shouldn't be a sommelier." My lips twitch into a smile. I smush a cheese crumb between my fingertip and the board, lifting it up to suck it off my finger and accidentally making eye contact with Arjun as I do. I glance down at my wineglass, my face hot.

"And all I know about you is your name, a few family details, where you live, and that you'd be a terrible criminal," he says, and I flick my eyes up to see his smile.

A wave of desire rolls through me at that smile. *I gotta slow down on the wine.*

He pours more wine into his glass and offers to refill mine, but I shake my head, covering the rim. "My favorite color is green," he says after taking a long sip, "but the kind of green you see outside, not anything made up by a crayon company. I'm an only child, but I have thirteen cousins, and I'm the only male cousin."

"Oh my god."

"Yeah, it defies science."

"I think they make *Marvel* movies about you."

"I try not to reveal that until at least the fourth date."

I lean back in my chair, crossing my arms then uncrossing them. *Date?* I drain my glass, clutching it in my hand.

"I was born and raised in the Denver area," he continues. "When I graduated high school I went to culinary school in France but fell in love with cheese while I was there. I stayed in France for a few years and eventually moved back to Colorado to be closer to my family, and voilà. That's me."

"France? Like, Le Cordon Bleu France?" France seems like a place for prestigious, snobby chefs, not this down-to-earth cheese shop guy.

"Same country. Different school."

"Do you speak French?"

"I can hold a conversation."

"You know, if you want to impress a girl, maybe start there."

"And here I thought my extensive wine knowledge would do the trick."

"Almost."

Our smiles linger on each other for a beat longer than they should.

"Your turn," he says.

"I was born and raised in Texas, where my sister still lives. My parents sort of still live there—they're retired and have been cruise-ship-hopping all year. I went to school at Pennsylvania State College outside of Lancaster, Pennsylvania and then lived in Philly for the past eight years with my ex." The room starts to feel too small. I tilt my glass back and forth, watching the last drop of wine at the bottom of the glass shift around. My chest aches and my stomach feels tight. I didn't even say Ben's name, but just the mention of him conjures pain. It's a magic trick I didn't mean to learn.

"Eight years is a long time to spend with someone," he says, the tenderness in his voice sending a wave of sadness through my body.

I don't trust myself to talk quite yet, so I let silence stretch between us for a few seconds before answering. "We were actually together for twelve years—we just didn't move in together until after college." My voice comes out cracked and quiet.

He nods, acknowledging me. "You left out a detail though," he says.

I left out a lot of details, but I doubt I'll be sharing any of them. I'm about to tell him this, but he speaks before I can.

"You never told me your favorite color."

I raise my eyes to meet Arjun's and see a deep understanding there. He isn't passing over what I said; he's giving me an out. I'm not sure I'm ready to continue this conversation with him, so I gratefully take the exit ramp.

"Right, yeah." I half-smile, and the tension in my chest eases. "It doesn't exist."

"What do you mean?" he asks, leaning in.

"My favorite color is a mix. It doesn't exist anywhere except in my mind. And my paintings. It's sort of a teal color, but it's hard to describe. You'd have to see it."

"You'll have to show me sometime."

His face is so open and honest I don't think he's saying that just to say it.

"Only if you feed me again."

"You have yourself a deal."

At the mention of food my stomach groans, reminding me cheese and wine do not a dinner make. "Well, I think I'm going to head home, but thank you for all this." I gesture to the wine-glasses and cheese board.

"Anytime. And I mean that. Whenever you want cheese or wine, I'm your man."

My stomach flutters at those last three words. *Jesus, Mara, get a grip.* "And you let me know if you're hiring for the front counter," I say as I don my jacket.

His laugh echoes in his wineglass as he drains the contents.

"Do you have any plans this weekend?" he asks as he walks me to the door.

"Nope." I stand with my back against the door, facing him. He tucks his hands in his jean pockets and I mirror him, tucking my hands in my own.

"Fall Fest is on Saturday—would you be interested in going with me?"

The truth is, I would like to spend more time with Arjun. I was nervous about doing this, but it was a far better way to spend a few hours than alone in my cabin.

"One question: what is Fall Fest?"

"Only the single greatest culinary experience on this side of America," Arjun says.

"That is quite an endorsement. My expectations will be unmanageable."

"Is that a yes?" There's that hopeful ask again. When was the last time someone seemed eager to spend time with me like this?

"Sure."

His smirk turns into a full smile—a small shift that makes my stomach feel fluttery.

Why is my stomach fluttery?

"I could text you the details, but I'd need your number," Arjun says, slipping his phone out of his back pocket.

This man. "Smooth," I say, and my smile feels out of control. I give him my number, push against the door, and walk out into the cold.

If someone told me a month ago I'd be sharing a wineglass and cheese board with a cute guy tonight I would have given them a funny look. I thought for sure I wouldn't even be able to look at a guy for at least a year after my breakup, but Arjun's eyes and the sound of his laugh flash in my mind and the undeniable dip in my stomach happens. I don't know about a relationship, but I know for damn sure I'm ready to see his smile again.

7

"*I* absolutely will not be putting that in my mouth," I say, pointing to the pumpkin spice cotton candy Arjun holds out to me.

We've been at Fall Fest for almost an hour and I've lost count of the number of foods he's handed me. I remember the bourbon kettle corn, candied squash, and a candied bacon, apple, Gouda, and Brussels sprout sandwich, but everything else runs together in my mind. I've been pretty adventurous, but pumpkin spice cotton candy is where I draw the line.

Berkeley Park is normally home to families with small kids, runners doing loops on the two-mile path, and dog owners playing in the dog park, but tonight it belongs to Fall Fest. Booths of all kinds fill the park as far as the eye can see, and all of Copper Springs is out tonight.

Early October is a beautiful time to be in Colorado. There's a chill in the air that requires a coat, but the first snow hasn't hit yet. The air smells like all the things I've eaten tonight and more: popcorn, sugared apples, and smoked meat. A local band plays on a stage somewhere in the park, the sound drifting through the festival and mingling with the pings and dings at the game booths and the sizzles and splashes in the food tents. I was nervous about this non-date/date thing, but I've been having fun. Arjun has this way of making me feel like I'm the most important person in the world. I wonder if everyone feels like this with him.

"Don't think too hard about it." Arjun pulls off a small piece of the burnt orange wisp and holds it out to me. When I shake my head, he puts the sugar cloud in his mouth. "You gotta trust me on this one."

"You said that about the last three foods."

"And have I steered you wrong yet?"

"I like pumpkin exactly where it belongs—in a pie or a latte."

Arjun tears off another piece from the paper stick and holds it out to me. I push his hand away and scrunch my nose. The cotton candy starts to disintegrate on his finger, and he sticks this piece in his mouth too. I lead us away from the booth, eager to see more things. If Fall Fest existed when I was a kid, I was never in town for it. Summers and Christmases had their own fun festivities—it's the best part of small-town life—but none were fall-themed.

Arjun stops abruptly in front of a basketball game booth. The booth is empty save for a gangly teenager who looks like he'd rather be anywhere else than here. The game is one of those moving target basketball games, and stuffed animals of varying sizes and colors cover the side walls of the booth.

"All right, I wasn't going to use this card, but you've left me no choice. If you try this pumpkin spice cotton candy, I'll win you a huge teddy bear."

I snort-laugh. "How big, exactly?"

Arjun points to the massive pink teddy bear at the top of one of the side walls. He raises his eyebrows and holds out the cotton candy stick to me.

"You drive a hard bargain, but you have yourself a deal," I say as I pull off a wisp of the sweet cloud and stuff it in my mouth.

Arjun's face lights up in anticipatory excitement. "Well . . .?"

"Okay, it was weirdly delicious. You were right. Again."

"Yes! See? I told you!" He grabs my upper arm and squeezes it. "Now I'm going to win you a stuffed animal."

I've lost track of how much time I've spent smiling tonight. My cheeks hurt and I feel like I need to be tethered to the earth so I don't float away. I forgot how fun it could be to flirt. Not to mention Arjun's playfulness and delight over this festival is absolutely contagious.

He approaches the game booth, handing me the cotton candy before paying the grumpy teenager who hands him a basketball. The teenager explains that Arjun gets five tries to get the ball in the hoops, and if he sinks them all he can pick out the prize he wants. Arjun readies his stance and with the grace of an athlete launches the ball into the net. Loud dings radiate from the booth, the sound of a winner.

"Woo! One down, four to go!" I shout, clapping awkwardly because of the cotton candy stick in my hands.

He looks over his shoulder at me, his face beaming with pride. When he sinks the ball one, two, three more times, each time I cheer a little louder. On the fifth shot he sets up just like he did for the other four, but the target moves just as he tosses the ball and a buzzer sounds off, letting everyone within earshot know he missed. He slumps, defeated, but when he turns to me his face is still bright with joy. Arjun haggles with the teenager, who points to the small and medium-sized stuffies. Arjun points to a bright orange cat, which the teenager promptly hands to me.

"Now I'm a proper Fall Fest attendee," I say, the cat tucked under my arm, my fingers sticky from the cotton candy. I chuck the empty stick in a nearby garbage can while Arjun and I resume our walk through the grassy paths.

"You look like one. Though you might need a beer to complete the look. Shall we?"

"Only if you let me buy."

"Now who's driving a hard bargain?" He elbows me, teasing.

I elbow him back, unable to contain my smile. We've been acting like teenagers all night, and I feel like one too. Arjun is fun, and I haven't felt this alive in a long time.

"So how long are you in town?" he asks, tucking his hands into his jacket pockets.

"I'm not sure, actually. I—"

"Arjun!" a voice calls, interrupting.

Both Arjun and I turn in the direction of the voice. A few booths away, two girls wave madly from their table, which is piled high with books. He waves back, and we head toward them.

"Who are those girls?" I ask, suddenly a little nervous.

"Olive and Indy. Olive owns the bookshop on Main Street, and Indy sells cookies. We're all part of a networking group for local small business owners. They're great—you'll like them."

We're at the table before I can ask any more questions. The table itself is half-covered with cookies and half-covered with books stacked as high as I am tall. A bright pink tablecloth sits under it all with two signs in the front.

Olive Books @IndyCookieQueen

Adorable cookies decorated like pumpkins, ghosts, and apples in a cute cartoon style line the cookie side of the table.

"Wow, these are amazing." I pick up one of the ghost cookies in its plastic wrapper.

"Thank you," the taller of the two girls says. She's got bright blonde hair cut just under her chin and wears a mustard-yellow sweatshirt that says "Cookie Queen" with a bright red puff jacket. "I'm Indy. I don't think we've met."

"Mara." I try to play it cool—as much as I can holding a stuffed cat toy.

"She's new in town," Arjun says, and the girl next to Indy sticks out her hand for me to shake next.

"I'm Olive. Have you been by Olive Books yet? We're really close to Arjun's bistro."

"I haven't, but I promise I will soon."

Dimples appear on Olive's freckled cheeks. Her cinnamon-red hair is reed straight and cut similar to Indy's, giving them an air of closeness, like sisters. It's clear the two are close friends, and a pang of longing for my ex-best friend Blair hits me square in the chest.

"Indy, where do you sell your cookies?" I reach for my purse to pay for the ghost cookie I'm holding, but she puts her hand on mine.

"That's on me. Friend of Arjun discount." She winks. "I sell on Instagram though. You can follow me @IndyCookieQueen." She points to the sign on the front of the table.

I make a mental note and tuck the cookie into my purse. "Thank you, that's so nice."

"This is Indy's clever marketing strategy. One freebie, then you're selling a kidney to get more," Arjun says.

"Oh, it's so true," Olive agrees.

Indy blows a raspberry. "It works almost as well as Arjun's

marketing strategy, which is just to be ridiculously good-looking."

Arjun rolls his eyes, and Indy gives him a teasing look.

"You don't sell these in your shop, do you?" I ask Arjun, not missing the way Indy's gaze lingers on him a little longer.

"No, he does not," Indy says. She sounds playfully indignant, and Arjun gives her a good-natured eye roll. "But not for lack of trying."

"Listen, Indy's cookies are the real deal. They don't have a long shelf life. My crowd wouldn't take them fast enough to appreciate them," he says, and it sounds like he's given this speech before.

"Indy, don't harass Arjun in front of his date," Olive says.

"I'm not—" I stutter.

"Oh my god, Olive, you can't say things like that," Indy says, giving her a playful slap on the arm. "Look what you've done to poor Mara."

She slaps both hands over her mouth. "I'm so sorry," she says, sounding more like she broke my favorite lamp than called me Arjun's date.

"No no no, it's fine!" I say at the same time Arjun says, "It's fine, Olive."

We all laugh a bit awkwardly before Indy chimes in, saving the moment.

"Arjun, how was your meeting with that vineyard I told you about? Delicious, right?"

"I adore that place," Olive says, and they start to discuss people and places I don't know.

Small towns are the kind of place where you know people and they know you. I've seen it all night, clumps of people who are neighbors and friends greeting everyone who passes them by because there are no strangers here. But no one here knows me, save for Arjun and Dany, and in turn I know no one. Alone in my cabin this knowledge feels like freedom, but surrounded by so many people it feels like being trapped, and this conversation only twists the knife.

"Hey, sorry to interrupt." I turn to Arjun. "I'm just going to go to the face painting booth—I told Dany I'd stop by. I'll meet you there."

He nods, and I say my goodbyes to the girls, slipping away before anyone tries to convince me to stay.

As I make my way through the crowd, I pretend like I'm in a movie, a camera clearing the way and everyone ignores me because the point of the scene is to meet the heroine and hear her voiceover. I weave through clusters of people and dodge two groups of teenagers throwing candy at each other. I'm trying to decide on which Phoebe Bridgers song would best match this moment in the movie scene when a pair of waving arms catches my attention.

"Mara!" Dany shouts. She's standing and swinging her paint-covered arms over her head.

I wave and make a beeline for the face painting table she's running. A small girl with a freshly painted butterfly on her cheek runs past me as I approach.

"You found me," Dany says, standing and hugging me. That lonely feeling inside dissolves.

"I promised I would," I say.

Dany's table has all the fun, chaotic energy of her personality. It's covered in a sheet of brown kraft paper splattered with paint and water droplets. Paper towels, brushes, cups of water, and face paint palettes are scattered about, and I have a strong impulse to tidy it.

"Quite the operation you've got going here," I say, picking up the catalog of designs Dany can draw on people's faces and browsing the laminated pages. "This a popular booth?"

"Who doesn't love getting their face painted?" Dany gestures to her own face, which is painted with whimsical pastel blue-and-pink lines.

"Is that glitter?"

"It is definitely glitter. Also, would you mind?" She rinses out the brush she's been holding this whole time and hands it to me. "I gotta pee and I'm starving. I'll be right back."

"What am I—? Hang on a sec!"

"I'll be right back!" Dany shouts over her shoulder as she skips away. She's actually skipping. I'm starting to wonder if she's a fae child pretending to be an adult human.

There's a tug on my jacket. When I look down, the source of the tug smiles up at me with a gap-toothed grin.

"Can I have a Spider-Man face?" a young boy asks, plopping himself down on the chair opposite where I'm standing.

"I, um . . ." I flip through Dany's book to find the requested painting. Sure enough, in the back with the rest of the full-face spreads there's a Spider-Man face. "This one?" I ask, pointing to the photo, and the little boy nods vigorously.

My heart races. Despite the cooler temperature, I feel a little hot. I tuck my stuffed cat under the table, unzip my jacket, and sit in the chair Dany sat in, placing the open notebook close enough that I can copy what she's done.

It's just a face painting—there's no pressure. It's not a big deal. You are totally capable of painting a Spider-Man face.

I dip my brush into the blob of red paint in one of the paint palettes, exhale a shaky breath, and get to work. By the time I've finished I'm exhausted. My hands are shaky and sweaty, and I've convinced myself he's going to hate it.

"Are you done? Can I see?" he asks, and I hold up the small mirror Dany set out by the water cups. His smile bursts open the tightness in my chest. "Cool!" he screams and bolts out of the chair.

Within seconds another child has climbed onto it, an elementary school-aged girl asking for a flower on her cheek.

Another deep breath. Clean the brush. Dip the paint. Release the pressure to get it right.

With each child, each excited smile and thank-you from a child or parent, I relax a little more. They sit in the chair as fast as I can finish a painting, and I barely have time to wonder where Dany is, as I lose myself in the cheap paints and chubby cheeks.

"Is it weird if I say I'm enjoying watching you work?"

Arjun's voice behind me draws me out of the face-painting trance. I smile but don't break focus. I'm trying to draw a cat per the request of a young girl in a cat costume. It's all very meta.

"Maybe a little," I say, gently turning the face of the child in front of me and dipping a fresh brush in black paint.

"Okay then, I'll keep that to myself."

I see Arjun move in my peripheral. He stands to the side of me crossing his arms, his eyes on me making me light-headed.

"Is this what you're like when you're working?" he asks.

"When I'm capturing the realism of a cat's face with cheap paint? Yes."

Arjun laughs. It's a deep, genuine belly laugh. A shiver runs through my body, and I have to pause for a moment before finishing the painting.

I set down the brush and hold up the mirror. This child shouts a thank-you at me before running away.

"How did you get saddled with this?" Arjun asks, taking the seat across from me.

"Dany shoved a brush in my hand and ran away." I dip multiple brushes in the water cup, swirling them around, then drag them across a fresh paper towel to clean them. My muscles know this movement—it's as natural to me as breathing.

"She would," Arjun says, a chuckle in his voice. "All right, I'd like a slice of cheese painted on my face, please."

I set down the brushes and glare at him, but he turns his face and juts out his cheek. "I cannot paint a cheese slice."

"I thought you were a professional artist," he says.

"We all have our limits. What about a flower?"

"But cheese is my favorite!" he teases, petulant.

I've started to laugh, and that only spurs him on. He sticks out his lower lip, giving me an exaggerated sad face.

"I'm sorry! What about a balloon?"

Arjun sighs, big and dramatic. "All right," he says. "But I'm losing on the deal."

My cheeks ache from smiling. I dip a clean brush in the blue paint and take his face in my hand. The rough hair of his beard scratches my fingertips as I turn his head to the side. There's a small piece of fuzz from his scarf on his cheek, exactly where I need to paint, and I brush it away, the softness of his skin surprising me. I repeat the motion, unable to stop myself.

"Is there something . . .?"

"Oh, just a bit of fuzz." I snap my hand away from his face like a child caught with her hand in the cookie jar.

"Ah. Yes, you need a clean canvas."

I know I'm blushing, so I'm grateful his face is turned away from me.

I take my time with the miniature painting, luxuriating in

every small stroke and the way the brush glides against his skin. His proximity is dizzying, thrilling, as if I'm at the top of a roller coaster pitched forward, about to fall.

"How's it look?" Arjun asks when I set the paintbrush in the water cup.

"Like the best damn balloon I've ever painted."

He checks out my tiny painting in the mirror. "Incredible. I can't believe that was free."

"Next time you won't be so lucky."

"I'd say I got pretty lucky this time." He smiles at me, his eyes dancing, and the roller coaster drops.

8

I'm on the edge of sleep one night, days after Fall Fest, when bright blue paint and sepia skin flash in my mind. It's the first picture I've seen in in my mind in six months. My heart hammers in my chest and throat. *Is this real?* I clutch the blankets, waiting for the image to disappear, to leave me, but it doesn't. My fingers start to itch and colors swirl.

I nearly trip on my blankets in my sprint to the sunroom, almost knocking over the lamp while trying to turn it on. The living room wood stove won't heat this space, and I don't have time to build a fire, so I blast the space heater so I don't freeze. Like a goblin searching for treasure, I hunch over my box of paints, digging through them, desperation choking me. I don't know how long I have. I don't want to lose it. This is how my process has always started, with images and itchy fingers. I used to be filled to the brim with inspiration, my whole body carrying the weight of multiple projects. I forgot what this was like. What sweet relief to bear the burden of an idea again.

My paints are a mess and my hands won't stop shaking, so it takes me a long time to find the colors I'm looking for. Spreading my paints, a palette knife, and a hodgepodge of brushes on the floor, I kneel over my palette, buzzing with nervous energy as I start to mix the colors, matching them to the image still looming in my mind. The muscle memory of mixing paints comes back to me as if it never left at all.

I want to rejoice in this moment, scream it from the rooftops, celebrate with cake and champagne. *This is it! This is what I've been waiting for! My art has come back to me!* I'm going to be able to fill my exhibition with new pieces, sell those pieces, put money back in my bank account, and paint a commission piece that will bring in more money than I've ever made on anything. I could burst with joy.

I sit back on my heels admiring the colors I've mixed. I haven't lost my touch. If anything, I did that quicker than I ever have. There's only one canvas left that I haven't destroyed and I drag it over to my space on the floor. I'll buy an easel next time I'm in town. The idea of it makes me giddy, as if I just drank a gallon of bubbles and my blood is fizzing.

I'm ready to paint for the first time in way too long.

But as I go to dip the brush in the paint, I freeze. Suddenly, something feels very wrong. The image in my mind is gone, but the imprint of it is still there. It's like a word right on the tip of my tongue—I know it's there, but I can't seem to access it. I squeeze my eyes trying to conjure it, the brown skin, the brilliant blue, but nothing comes.

Oh god.

All my energy leaves me as if it's been drained from my body, and I drop my brush. The image that drove me to the floor of my sunroom disappears, and I'm left empty.

I slump to the ground, leaning against the couch, pressing my palms against my forehead as if it'll bring back the image, the inspiration, but nothing happens. That void where all the colors and ideas fleetingly lived inside my soul is gray once more. This is almost worse than it was before. A brief encounter with my old self only for it to be snatched from me is a cruelty I wouldn't wish on my enemies.

My chest aches, and I clutch at the fabric of my shirt as if I can get to my heart and squeeze it until all the hurt leaks out. Why can't I do this? I just used the charcoal pencil the other day. I thought it was evidence that my creativity is still alive inside of me, but maybe I was wrong.

A sob rips through the silence of the cabin, my body heaving as all the grief and sadness inside of me comes out. I thought maybe back in April, right after my breakup, all my misery was just over the loss of Ben, but I recognize the raw sorrow in my heart now and I haven't thought for one minute about my ex.

My phone dings from my bedroom. I have no concept of what time it is. It's as dark outside now as it was when I walked into the room, and I don't have a clue how long I've been in here. It has to be late though.

I dash the back of my hand across my eyes to try to clear them. My limbs are a hundred pounds each and somehow, I still manage to haul myself off the floor. The bed will be a more comfortable place to cry anyway. I tuck myself in after throwing an extra log into the wood stove in the living room. Then, buried under blankets, I let the weight of them comfort me as I check my phone. My eyes are still wet, and I blink away the blurriness. Charleigh's texted me a meme about living in Colorado. The edge of my lips tug, a weak attempt at a smile.

You're still up?

Had some work to finish up.

Yeah, you seem really busy.

This was a mental health break. Why are you still up?

I think about being honest, but just typing the words brings a fresh round of tears, so I delete them. I'm just not sure if Charleigh and I have fully repaired this thing between us. Before three years ago I wouldn't have hesitated to tell her, to ask if we could talk and spill my guts.

My phone vibrates in my hand. Charleigh is calling.

"Hi." I put her on speakerphone, laying the phone next to me on the pillow. The screen projects a dim glow, a spot of light in the inky black of my room.

"Hey, are you okay? I saw the blue dots and then they disappeared, and it's late, so I thought something might be wrong, but now I've called I realize I'm probably overthinking."

I snort. "For once, you did not overthink."

"You're not okay?"

"Not really," I say, but the words stick in my throat and it's hard to swallow. I let fresh tears stream sideways down my face and dampen my pillow.

"What happened?" The concern in Charleigh's voice, the absolute kindness and love, is too much.

My chin quivers, a fresh sob building inside. My sternum feels full, as if I've been holding my breath. "What if I never paint again?" I've said these words in my head many times, but never out loud. Never where the risk of an answer I don't want to hear is greater than the risk of not saying it at all.

"You'll paint again. I'm sure of it," she says.

"You have to say that—you're my sister."

"I'm no stranger to telling you things you don't want to hear."

The silence stretches between us. This is the closest we've come to talking about what happened between us after our grandparents' funeral. Now is not the moment for this, though, and we both know it.

"Why can't I paint, Charleigh?" My voice is thin and papery, straining against the emotion clogging my throat.

"I don't know, Mars Bar." She uses my childhood nickname, something she hasn't done in years. This sends me over the edge.

The bubble in my chest bursts, and I let out all the sorrow, all the fear, the emotions constantly swirling inside. Charleigh lets me cry for as long and hard as I need to. When the tears slow, I inhale and exhale shaky breaths until I feel I can form sentences again.

"I don't know who I am without my art, and I don't know how to be anyone else," I say when I can finally manage it.

"You don't have to be anybody else or learn to be anyone else. You're still healing. Give yourself time, Mara. You said you're in therapy, right? What does your therapist say about all this?"

"I *was* in therapy. For as long as I could afford it." I mumble the last part.

"What might your therapist say then? If you were in a session with her right now."

"You don't have to fix this, Charleigh."

"I'm not trying to, but you're swimming deep in your feels and you need to put your feet back on the ground."

"I like being deep in my feels," I say.

"I know. But just humor me for a second. What might your therapist say about all this?"

I tap my phone screen, which has been black for some time. The sudden brightness stings my sore eyes and I click it off again. My therapist, Ashley, saved me after my breakup. My weekly sessions with her are the reason I'm not still curled into a fetal position in a hotel room in Philly wracking up credit card debt. She guided me through the earliest, darkest days of my breakup and encouraged every step of my healing. She understood when I had to stop seeing her for financial reasons—therapy isn't cheap without insurance—but by then I was feeling a little more steady anyway.

"I think she'd tell me it's okay that I don't know who I am right now. That I should try to be curious about it. And maybe I should try to explore what that means, like . . . who I am right now while I'm not painting."

Charleigh hums a sound of understanding, of agreement.

Thinking of Ashley now, I miss her wisdom and guidance. One more reason I'm eager to paint again and make money: I'd like to be able to afford therapy. Especially for moments like this. But Charleigh will have to do.

"I would agree with all of that," she says. "And I would just add that you don't have to know who you are right now, or believe in yourself, or have much hope, because I do. And I have enough for both of us."

"Thank you," I say, sleep pulling at me. My eyelids are gummy and heavy. "When did you get to be so wise?"

"It's an older sister thing."

As teenagers Charleigh and I would have knock-down, drag-out fights and twenty minutes later drive to McDonalds for French fries, blasting the Spice Girls and sing-screaming every word. This is the beauty of having a sister—the unspoken agreement that harsh words can be forgotten and deep wounds healed.

"Good night, Charleigh."

"Good night, Mara."

I convinced myself Charleigh wouldn't want to fix what was broken between us, that the valley was too deep, the bridge too burned. I was sure the path we found ourselves on was too far gone and we'd never find our way back. And maybe we'll never be what we once were. But here we are, maps torn and taped together, compasses in hand, not retracing our steps but forging a new path, together.

9

I know as soon as I wake up the morning after my paint failure that I need to get out of the house, so I yank on my hiking boots and layer up with a puff jacket, hat, and gloves. I leave my phone behind and hit the trail behind my cabin.

When Charleigh and I were young, Grampy cleared a path from the cabin to a local trail so we could access it easily. He chopped down the trees and cleared the brush, walking the trail himself as often as he could so we could enjoy easy access to a nice hike. The trail isn't well-known to visitors, but locals like it. It doesn't lead to any vistas—it's just a path through the woods. It's never truly crowded, but I'm hoping it's empty today.

A thin layer of mostly melted snow covers the ground, left over from a small October storm. My boots crunch against the icy path. The steady thrum of my heartbeat and my breath loud in my ears work in tandem to soothe all the raw patches of me exposed by my failure last night. The smell of dirt, snow, and evergreen pine needles is a balm for my aching soul.

Before my breakup I knew exactly who I was. Mara West,

long-time partner of Ben Moorehouse, daughter to James and June, sister to Charleigh, aunt to Alice, artist. I got to do what I loved for a living. I never felt lost. I always knew exactly who I was and where I was going.

I hadn't spoken to Charleigh in years by the time Ben betrayed me and my creativity dried up. Those early months I was so lost. No sister, no partner, no art. My parents had just jumped on a cruise ship to tour the world for a year. I spent most of my days watching and rewatching *Buffy the Vampire Slayer* while eating microwave meals. Jackie dragged me out a few times, mostly to museums, but that was more painful than helpful, and eventually she got the hint and just took me for drinks instead. Ashley, my therapist, was the one who helped me regain my sense of self and see that I could be more than just a shell of myself, that I could heal, even without being able to paint. I've figured out who I am without Ben, but there's still a piece of me missing. I know I'll get it back when I can paint again. I know it's all I need to feel whole again.

But how do I get it back? How do I get past whatever's blocking me? Is it what Charleigh and Jackie and Dany all said— that it's just a matter of time, of believing in myself and trying over and over again? Or maybe I just need to let go and wait for my art to come back to me.

Do I even have time for that?

Ahead of me I hear footsteps on the trail, accompanied by the panting of a dog and the jingle of a collar. When it becomes clear I'm going to cross paths with the person I step off the trail and onto the side, burying my face in my scarf. I mumble a hello as they approach, hoping it will suffice, but a big black dog stops to sniff at my legs. Instinctively, I lean over, trying to keep its face out of my crotch.

"Hi. Oh shit, I'm sorry," says a familiar voice.

My head snaps up.

"Bear, stop it— Mara?"

"Arjun? Hi."

"I forgot you knew about this trail," he says, a wide smile on his face.

"One of my favorites."

The dog jumps up on me, his paws punching my stomach, and I grunt. I'd hoped not to see anyone today, but this is a pleasant surprise. I admit I've been thinking about Arjun quite a bit since Fall Fest last week.

"Bear, come on. She doesn't want you all over her." Arjun lunges forward, but I wave him off.

"She doesn't mind," I say with a smile and squat down to Bear's level. I scratch behind his ears and let him lick my face. This is just the kind of joy I need today. "Is this your dog?"

"He's one of my cousins'. Just pet sitting for the day."

"Cheese shop not open today?" I stand and brush off my jacket.

Bear sniffs around my feet, finding a stick to gnaw on.

"It is, but I hand over the reins to my cafe manager at least once a week. Waste of living in Colorado if I'm inside all the time."

"I'm sure your girlfriend appreciates you taking time away," I mumble into my scarf, avoiding eye contact and readjusting my gloves.

I'm pretty sure he's single considering the way he flirts with me, but I saw the way Indy looked at him last weekend. He might be dating around. Not that I'm interested in a relationship or anything, but it seems like a good thing to know. Just in case.

"No girlfriend," he says with a knowing smile. "And frankly, I'm not even sure my ex would have noticed."

"Ex? I'm sorry. I didn't mean to . . ."

"We broke up for the last time about a year ago. She was a piece of work." He rolls his eyes, and the smile on his face is one of annoyance, not pleasant nostalgia. "I'm sorry. You came out for a hike, not to hear about my ex. I'll let you get back to it."

"No, no, I like it. I mean, I don't mind." My tongue feels too big for my mouth and I can't seem to get my words right. I do want to hear about his ex. I want to hear everything he'll tell me about himself and his life. But apparently I've forgotten how to string a full sentence together when the full weight of Arjun's attention is on me.

"Any plans for the rest of the day?" Arjun whistles, patting his thigh. Bear thumps his tail against the ground and hops up, ditching his stick for whatever exciting plans his human must have.

"This walk was my big plan. How 'bout you?"

"Maybe a warm beverage with a beautiful stranger . . .?" he says casually, brushing the snow and dirt off Bear's coat and glancing up at me.

I bite my bottom lip and try to stop the smile from creeping onto my face. "I thought we agreed on acquaintance?"

* * *

Bear seems just as excited to be going inside as he was to meet me on the trail, probably anticipating whatever food or treats await him. I too am looking forward to treats. A hot drink and Arjun's company may be just what I need after today.

The cabin is warm, and Arjun's already started to shed layers by the door when I step in. He hangs his jacket on a hook and starts to pull his sweater over his head, but his T-shirt gets caught in the sweater, lifting with it. More than a flash of skin, half his torso is exposed, and my breath catches in my throat. I need to look away, but his rich brown skin is the most perfect color, and there's no way I got it right when I mixed that color yesterday. With some effort I avert my eyes, but all the textures of him, the muscles and soft curves, they linger in my mind.

"Feel free to hang your stuff here too," he says, pointing to the rack and pulling his shirt down without a hint of self-consciousness.

I blink a few times, bringing myself back to reality, before tucking my hat and gloves into my pockets and hanging my jacket on the hook next to his.

His cabin is laid out similarly to mine, a large open space split between a kitchen and a quaint living room. A wood stove nestled against the wall by a couch and a couple of recliners heats the space, just like my cabin. Instead of two side bedrooms, though, he's got just one in the back, the door slightly ajar. It's smaller than my cabin but just as cozy. The heat of the stove calls to me, and I oblige after pulling off my hiking boots.

Bear follows me but hops up on the couch, curling up on a pile of blankets.

The whole cabin smells the way Arjun usually does—faintly of woodsmoke. But there are notes of cumin and wine and yeast in the air as if whatever he ate for dinner last night became today's air freshener.

"Did you decorate the place yourself?" I ask over my shoulder. The walls are bare, but the pillows, rug, and blankets all have a color scheme. The whole place looks like it belongs in a magazine or on a Pinterest board—something I did not expect from a bachelor cabin.

"I did, though I'd hardly call it decorating. I know the walls in here are empty, but I do have a painting—it just looks better in my bedroom. Tea, coffee, or hot chocolate?"

"Coffee, please. Black. So you've got a painting, huh?" Sufficiently thawed out, I join Arjun in the kitchen.

He pours boiling water into the French press and sets the lid on top. "I thought you'd be interested in that," he says with a chuckle, brushing his hands on his jeans. "Here, I'll show you."

He leads me to the back of the cabin and through the door. I hesitate for a moment before stepping in but decide if he's not going to be weird about it, I'm not either. My eyes are drawn to his king-size bed, sheets rumpled from when he last slept in it. I force myself not to stare at it though—not to conjure images of his bare torso—and turn my attention to the painting.

It takes me a second to register what I'm looking at, but I finally see it. It's one of mine. It's a painting of the sky with just the tips of the trees at the bottom, like someone was trying to take a picture of some trees but their camera accidentally tilted up at the last second. Something I actually did that inspired this painting. It's as many shades of blue as I could discover and fit onto the canvas with just a hint of darker green at the bottom. The gold frame he's used for it is perfect, accentuating every hue.

"It's stunning, isn't it?" he asks, awe in his voice.

"It is." I peek at him.

Arjun looks at my painting the way he might look at a beautiful woman, and I feel it in my core because to me what he's admiring is a piece of my soul. To be gazed at so lovingly, even just through my art, makes my chest ache. I should tell him it's mine. This is the perfect moment to do it. But the thought of it makes me cold and tingly. I don't think I can. Not yet.

"You probably recognize the artist," he says.

"Um, well, yes." It's not a lie.

"It's Dany's favorite artist, M. North. Sorry, I assume you artist types know all the famous artists. I was stereotyping," he says around an awkward chuckle.

My relief is so great my laugh comes out strangled and too loud. I thought for a minute he was going to out me, pull back the curtain and expose the woman behind it. But there was none of that.

I clear my throat. "Well, it suits the room really well," I say.

"I thought so too. Dany recommended the artist. Not cheap, but certainly worth it."

I admire my own work, nostalgic for the version of myself who painted this. That girl was drowning in images and had more ideas than time in the day. Creativity oozed from her fingers and joy accompanied every late-night work session. She feels like the alternate universe version of me.

"What do you think of it?" he asks, looking at me now. "Like, what does the painting do for you? Make you think of? Are those the right questions, or am I embarrassing myself?"

His earnestness brings me so much joy I let out a breathy laugh. "What do I think of it? It's your painting. What do YOU think of it?"

"But you're an artist, and I want your thoughts."

No one's ever asked me about my own art like this. When I attended my own galleries, I did so as a stranger in the crowd. Jackie and I talk about my art, but this is different. This spotlight is strange. It's another opportunity to come clean, to tell him who I am, but the cold feeling returns.

I'll tell him later.

"It makes me think of accidental beauty. You know when you look at something you see all the time with fresh eyes, and suddenly that thing is so beautiful you can't believe how lucky you are that you get to see it every day? That's what this painting reminds me of."

"I like that. I sometimes feel that way about this painting. One day it's the painting I've stared at every day for the past year, and the next day I forget how to breathe when I look at it. To me it feels like home. It's like I'm being invited to expand and explore, but to always come home."

I adjust my posture, feeling taller. Hearing him talk about my art this way fills me with a deep satisfaction, the kind only brought on by true admiration and understanding of my work. Ben never engaged with my work like this, commented on it or even complimented it. In the early years he'd feign interest, but he later told me he didn't actually care for art. He said it wasn't anything personal, but that he just didn't get it. In the later years he only talked to me about my work to ask me how much a piece would go for or tell me he was glad I was done with a painting so I could "clean up after myself around the house for once." But Arjun's comments, the light in his eyes when talks about my work, scab over the open wounds left behind by Ben. I didn't even realize they were still open until now.

One day I'll tell him how this moment, this kindness, healed something in me.

"Coffee should be ready now," he says, his eyes darting to my lips and then back up, so subtle I might have imagined it.

I follow him out of the bedroom with just one glance back at my painting. And the bed.

"How long were you with your ex?" I ask. Thinking of Ben

reminds me of Arjun's comment about his ex. Though I've only known him for three weeks, I already know he's a better man than the one I spent twelve years with. *What kind of woman is dumb enough to let this one go?*

"We were on and off for four years." Arjun sets up our mugs on a side table between his couch and a recliner and gestures for me to take a seat. I claim the recliner and a mug, tucking my legs under me. Arjun sits on the end of the couch closest to me, one leg on the floor, the other semi-crossed over it.

"Four years? Wow. How did you guys meet?"

"Through a friend. Her name was Roshni and it should have ended after two years." He rubs his forehead like maybe he's got a headache coming on. "But I was like a puppy that doesn't know he's unwanted. We'd break up and she'd come back after a few months. Every time I was so happy, so relieved, cause when she'd leave, I was a mess. I just had no self-respect."

"Why the back-and-forth? Why leave at all if she just kept coming back?"

"I didn't know this for, like, two years, but she kept leaving me for someone else. I was living in Denver at the time, working at a deli during the day and a restaurant at night. I had weird hours and I'm not on social media, so my world was very small. It was just work and Roshni. But she'd dump me for another guy, and when it didn't work out, she'd come back. I had no idea, but apparently, I was always her plan B." He pinches his lips together, exhaling sharply, then runs a hand through his hair, mussing it so it sticks out in different directions.

He said they just ended things for good a year ago, but I can still see the hurt she caused him all over his face.

"But you eventually found out?"

"A buddy of mine told me what was going on. He saw her out

with another guy one night. And I should have ended it for real then, but I don't know, I was convinced I could make her love me the way I loved her. So for two more years I held on. I thought I could be everything she needed and she wouldn't want anyone else."

"Oh, Arjun." My hand rests over my heart, which aches for this sweet man.

He reaches over and pats Bear's back. The dog snuffles and thumps his tail against the couch. "I know. My cousins tell me all the time that I love and trust too easily."

"That's not always a bad thing," I say.

"It can be when it gets your heart broken." His eyes drop to his lap.

In lieu of words I make a sympathetic noise in the back of my throat. I know how it feels to have your heart smashed to bits by someone you thought loved you the way you loved them.

"But you probably know something about that," he says rather than asks, lifting his eyes to mine. The same openness is there that always is, but I see it differently now. Before, I saw someone ready to let anyone in, someone who could maybe love anyone. But now I see a man with some cracks in his heart, just as nervous as I am to bare it to someone new.

"I do," I say carefully.

"What happened with your ex?" he asks as if he knows the answer is sacred, only to be given to those worthy of hearing it.

"Um, well. He was . . . mean." It's the first time I've said it out loud to anyone. When I notice my hands are shaking, I grip my mug a little tighter and take a sip to steady myself. "He never, like, hit me or anything, but he said some really awful things. Especially toward the end of our relationship. And I guess I'm telling you all this because I know how it feels to stay with someone for longer than you should."

Arjun's eyebrows draw together. He offers me a small, pained smile of understanding.

"I just didn't know there was any other way to be in a relationship. We'd been together since we were eighteen, so I didn't think it was that bad." I swallow hard. I get the sense that maybe I should stop, maybe I shouldn't spill my guts to this man, but the floodgates have opened and I'm not sure I could stop if I wanted to. "Even when someone tried to tell me how bad it was I wouldn't listen. Charleigh confronted me at a Thanksgiving dinner a few years ago. She told me he was abusive and I had to leave. But I didn't want to hear that, you know? I actually stopped talking to her for three years after she said that." I shake my head. Sadness moves through me like the ocean during a storm with unrelenting waves that threaten to drown me. I stall with a gulp of coffee. I really should stop here, but it's not the whole story. And he was brave enough to share his, so I can be brave too. "I kind of convinced myself it was me and Ben against the world and no one really understood us. Except my best friend Blair. She understood. But that might have been because she was fucking my boyfriend."

Arjun groans. "Jesus, Mara."

"Yeah." The word comes out like a heavy sigh. "They're having a baby together, Ben and Blair. And they're living in the house I bought for me and Ben." I pause. "And I'm . . . here."

The storm overtakes me, and whatever tears were waiting to fall wait no more. Crying at someone else's house is usually my cue to leave. I set my almost empty cup of coffee on the table between us, but before I can move my hand away Arjun catches my hand in his.

"For the record, I'm glad you're here."

"Thank you," I say.

"You deserved better," he says.

"So did you."

The look that passes between us is one of understanding. Before today, I thought Arjun and I were in different places in life. He was happy and had his shit together, probably ready to date, while I was on the fence about it. But really, we're just two people doing our best to mend our broken hearts after giving them away to the wrong people.

"God, I'm sorry I'm crying. Sometimes I'm fine, and then sometimes it feels like it just happened yesterday, you know?"

"I do. I really do. Here, let me . . ." He goes into the kitchen and returns holding out a paper towel, wincing as he says, "I don't have any tissues, sorry."

"Thank you." I accept the paper towel and clean my face of tears. "I should probably get home."

"Do you want a ride?" Arjun asks as I pull my shoes and coat back on.

"No, I'm happy to walk. Wouldn't want to disturb Bear anyway."

The dog snores loudly as if to punctuate my point.

"Sorry to cry all over your house," I say. "I'd tell you I'm not usually so emotional, but this is actually exactly who I am."

"I like who you are."

My heart swells.

Before I can overthink whether or not we should hug, Arjun moves forward and wraps his arms around me. I lean my head against his chest, listening to the sound of his heartbeat. He feels exactly the way I thought he would: sturdy and safe.

Later, as I'm walking back home, it occurs to me I don't have a vulnerability hangover. There's a distinct lack of self-loathing for having opened up to someone—to Arjun. I pause on the trail, realizing something else is stirring inside me. Desire. Not just the kind of desire that made me notice his bed, but the desire to share more. To tell him more about me and my life and hear more about his.

I wait for the pang of guilt to accompany all this, but nothing comes. All that's inside me is a yearning for more and the excitement of a girl with a crush on a boy.

10

Halloween on Main Street is a sight to behold. Golden yellow and crimson leaves dot the trees and litter the ground, every store window is packed with decorations: skulls, spiderwebs, skeletons, cauldrons, lights, and motion-activated monsters meant to scare people as they pass by. Even The Artist's Outlet has a decorated store window. Soft purple fairy lights strung across the top of the window hang over a display of two skeletons—one posing, the other painting. The painting skeleton wears a beret and holds a palette and brush, and there's a canvas set on an easel off to the side. The posing skeleton is arranged like "The Thinker" sculpture by Rodin. Painted on the small canvas is an unfinished portrait of the posing skeleton. It's been on display all month, and every time I've come by the portrait is painted a little more, as if the skeleton has been working on the painting throughout the month and now, the day before Halloween, the portrait is almost done. It's the best storefront in town.

The store is empty, as usual. I like a quiet space, but I hope it isn't a reflection of the store's financial status. Inside I browse the aisles, picking out an easel and another canvas. I'm not hopeful I'll have another flash of inspiration like I did a couple weeks ago, as I haven't had one since, but if I do I want to be ready.

I set my goodies on the counter and peek around the space for Dany. I don't see her, but I do hear humming from beyond the open door behind the counter. Leaving my things, I venture toward the noise into a back room. But it turns out the back room isn't a back room at all—it's a large studio. It's like walking through a wardrobe to find an entirely new world. Like some kind of Art Narnia. The space feels huge, though in reality it's not much larger than her store. The floor is concrete and covered randomly in drop cloths. There's an unfinished feel to the room. All the walls are concrete too except for one. The back wall isn't a wall at all but windows overlooking a stunning panoramic view of the mountains. In a semicircle of drawing tables set up in the middle of the studio, I find Dany setting supplies at each station, humming like no one's listening.

"Holy shit," I say, completely in awe.

Dany yelps and clutches at her chest. "Oh my god, you scared me."

"I'm so sorry." I half-giggle. "I seem to have a habit of doing that."

"I scare easily. Probably all those true crime podcasts." She resumes doling out supplies to each station.

I'm about to ask her what all this is for when a painting across the room catches my eye. I walk toward it for a closer look. It's the view outside the studio windows, painted in a way that's so realistic I could hold it up to the window and it would line up perfectly.

"This is really good, Dany," I say. "Who did this?"

96

."Me. It's still a work-in-progress." She keeps her back to me, her voice quiet and nonchalant.

"It's really impressive. I know you said drawing was your thing, but you're no newbie with a brush."

She joins me over at the painting. "That makes me feel better. Honestly. It's for a contest, and I'm just . . . I don't know. I kind of hate it."

"Hate it? What do you hate?"

"I don't even think I could put my finger on it exactly. I might just be at that point where I've spent too many hours with it. You know what I mean, right?"

I snort. "Alas, the creative cycle. You'll come around again."

"I'd love your thoughts on it. Any feedback?"

Asking for feedback is a vulnerable thing, and Dany obviously trusts me. If it didn't make my stomach clench with guilt I'd want to savor this moment. This is the kind of connection I've longed for with a friend, but not being known in art circles has kept me from this privilege. When I study her painting, I push away the shadow of my secret. I'm going to be the kind of friend Dany deserves even if it's just for these brief minutes, one artist to another.

"So I think you picked a great palette. The colors completely evoke the feeling of looking out that window. Out of any window, really, and seeing nature. I think you're bringing the viewer outside. You might want to look at where the eye is being drawn though." I gesture to the bottom of the painting where the trees are. She's painted them in such a way that I can practically feel the pine needles in my hands. "You've got a lot of detail here, and not as much up here." I gesture to the top of the mountain range. "So I don't know how much of a critique this is, but I'd spend more time on this top part."

Dany nods vigorously, turning to me with bright, shiny eyes. "You know what? That was my instinct too, but I thought, no, no, I've worked on that part for so long I'm sure it's fine. But I bet that's . . ." She trails off, scrutinizing the painting, then snaps out of it with a sharp inhale. "Okay, yes. So many ideas. Thank you!"

"Anytime," I say, and I mean it. Maybe enough good deeds will give me some favor in her eyes when I eventually tell her the truth about M. North.

"Sorry, I didn't even ask why you were here. Do you need anything? I'm, like, the worst store owner ever," she says with a laugh.

"Actually, I am here to buy a couple supplies."

"Really! Are you painting?" Dany's eyes go wide.

"Not yet, but I thought I'd have the supplies on hand just in case." Not in the mood to relive my paint failure two weeks ago, I change the subject. "What's going on in here?" I gesture to the setup.

"Drawing class! There's a live model tonight. You should come." She winks, not so subtly.

"Why?" I furrow my brow at her, narrowing my eyes.

"You miiiiight know the model." She shrugs her shoulders up in an exaggerated way and walks through the studio back into the store.

"Is it Arjun?" I follow her, my stomach lurching into my throat.

"Maybe," she says over her shoulder.

I lean against the counter as she rings up my items, considering her invite but also my bank account. "How much is the class?"

"First one is free." She smiles and takes my credit card, running it through the system and handing it back to me. "Bag?"

I shake my head. Twisting my ring around my finger, I don't move to leave yet. Without the excuse of money I don't really have a reason to say no. It's not as if I have any plans tonight, just another evening of glaring daggers at my paint supplies, rewatching Seinfeld on my phone, and falling asleep too late.

"When does it start?"

"In an hour." Dany tidies the register, contained excitement written all over her face. "Plus, I bet it will help get you unstuck from painting."

"If I can't paint, how are you so sure I can draw?"

She looks thoughtful for a moment. "I guess I'm not, but sometimes a different medium can spark something. Usually when I'm stuck I just go for a walk or watch a movie, and I can come back to the thing I was working on and *boom*, unblocked. But sometimes I have to switch projects to get unstuck. Sometimes I have to switch mediums entirely. One time I was working with watercolor, painting the view out back. I was kind of trying to emulate that M. North painting." She gestures to my painting above her fireplace, and my stomach clenches. "And I got *so* stuck even though I was using another painting as a guide. I tried charcoal, pastels, acrylics, oils, crayons, and then, as a Hail Mary, I tried paper-mache. Paper-mache! But it worked. And it's worked for a lot of my students. Might be worth a try."

I've heard this advice before, of course. I half-attempted it a couple months after the breakup when Ashley suggested it to see if it would help awaken any of my creative energy. I bought a blank sketchbook and a few drawing pencils, but the notebook is still blank all these months later, the pencils still perfectly sharp.

But Dany was right about the fireplace and she guided me through that. Although the idea makes me a little nauseated, I see no harm in trusting her again.

"All right, count me in."

"Yes!" Her face is triumphant, and she pumps her fist into the air.

"Can I help you get set up?"

Dany nods, her eyes shining. She stores my items behind the counter and leads me back into the studio, where I claim a station, hanging my jacket and purse over a chair. The sun starts to set as we set up a table for snacks and wine, painting the room in oranges and pinks. We turn on lamps placed around the room to enhance the soft overhead lighting at each drawing table station. Each desk has a desktop easel stacked with a few sheets of drawing paper, and while Dany gives the floor a final sweep, I straighten the chairs and pencils. Anything to distract me from the fluttery feeling in my stomach.

Eventually, people start to trickle into the studio, peeling off layers and loading small plates with cheese cubes and crackers. Many of the students seem to know each other, and they talk among themselves as Dany floats around to each person, chatting with them extensively before moving onto the next. A lady with a full head of long gray hair leaves her stuff at the station next to mine, nods a polite hello at me, and makes a beeline for the wine and cheese.

There's no sign of Arjun yet or anyone I know. I twist my ring around my finger, my heart hammering in my chest. I'm going to need alcohol to make it through this. But as I walk toward the snack table, my station neighbor walks up holding out a glass of white wine.

"You look like you might need this," she says.

"That obvious, huh?" I take a sip immediately, the cool drink a welcome texture to my dry mouth.

"I know the look of a woman who needs a glass of wine." She sets her glass on the drawing table and holds out a hand. "Ethel."

"Mara."

We shake hands and take our seats.

"How long have you been taking art classes?"

"I started art classes many years ago. I was a lawyer back in the day and I never did a damn creative thing in my life. But when I retired, I was determined to do it all. Been to every class Dany has here—sculpting, painting, you name it. I'm no good, but damn if I don't love it."

I used to have that kind of joy for art. I'm sure I lost it somewhere around the time I had to start turning in my work for grades. She's in the puppy love stage, and I feel like someone who's been married to art for decades right on the brink of a divorce. But her obvious passion stirs something inside me.

"How 'bout you? I haven't seen you around here before. This isn't your first class, is it?"

I'm not even sure where to start, or how to explain why I'm here, or how much I should share at all. But before I can answer the weight of a hand comes to rest on my shoulder. The source of the hand makes my stomach do that flippy thing.

"Arjun," I say. "Hi." *Did he get more handsome since the last time I saw him?*

I stand, and he steps toward me, closing the small gap between us. His arms wind around my waist as I close my arms around his shoulders. His breath is warm against my neck and his scent wraps itself around me as much as his arms do. His embrace is strong, his hand splayed out on my back. It lasts for one second and it lasts for a thousand.

"I didn't know you'd be here," he says, still halfway holding me in his arms.

"Dany invited me. She told me you were the model. I mean, that's not why I agreed. Well, it's sort of part of the reason—I just mean, okay, that's not . . ." *Fuck. What is wrong with me?*

The growing smile on Arjun's face makes my face heat. "It's nice to see you too," he says. His eyes drop to my lips, and my throat plunges to my stomach.

"Arjun!" Dany calls his name from across the room.

He releases me, but he's slow to look over at her, his gaze lingering on me for as long as possible, his head only turning as she approaches us.

"Thanks again for doing this. I owe you," Dany says.

"No way. I owe you for about five cheese-and-wine events. I'll be modeling for years to pay my debt to you," he says.

"Cheese-and-wine events?" I ask.

"Yeah, Arjun hosts these events at the store with all these different . . . well, cheeses and wines," Dany says with a giggle.

"The next one is in a month, right before Thanksgiving. You should come," Arjun says with a light touch on my upper arm. My skin tingles.

"Should we get started?" Dany asks Arjun.

He nods. "I'll catch you after class, okay?" Arjun gives my arm a gentle squeeze and walks away.

As I sit, I touch the place on my arm where his hand was. My skin itches for it to find my arm again.

"He's a looker, isn't he?" Ethel says.

I nod vaguely, but while Arjun and Dany chat at the front of the studio a thought occurs to me. "Ethel, this isn't a . . . nude drawing class, is it?" I keep my voice low and lean in so no one else can hear.

In art school we used models for drawing classes all the time, but usually our models were naked.

"God, I hope so." She winks at me, and I fight to keep my jaw from dropping.

Wait, does that mean there's a chance it is? Dany would have warned me if that was the case, right? And this is a community event— surely she wouldn't ask just anyone to get nude for a community painting class. Would she?

Suddenly, I feel very hot.

"All right, everyone, we're going to get started." Dany's voice raises above the low din.

Chairs squeak against the floor as people settle into their stations. Dany introduces Arjun and starts to give some instructions, reminders about what they've learned, but I don't hear any of it. My eyes are fixed on Arjun, waiting for him to start removing his clothes. He glances around the room, and when his eyes land on me he winks. My heart races.

But then Dany finishes her talk and turns on some instrumental music to play quietly over a Bluetooth speaker, and Arjun is still fully clothed. He reclines in the fold-up chair as best he can, hands resting in his lap. Everyone else has picked up their pencils and begun to sketch except for me. I'm still trying to recover from the sheer panic of what never ended up happening.

I wipe my palms on my jeans. Sweaty hands won't serve me.

Staring at the piece of paper in front of me, I pick up the provided pencil, twirling it in my fingers. I'm not entirely sure where to start. I sneak a glimpse at Ethel's paper. She's started on Arjun's head and neck, working top down, but the guy to my left has started with shoulders, arms, and torso. I drag my gaze back to Arjun and try to study him objectively, as an artist. It's nearly impossible because all I can think about is the way his black T-shirt hugs his shoulders, the way the veins in his hands display a secret strength, and how sturdy he felt in my arms,

I lick my lips, relishing the opportunity to drink him in unselfconsciously. I lean forward, resting my arms against the easel, but the weight of me tips it. I manage to catch it before it crashes to the floor, but the pencils drop, clattering on the concrete and scattering everywhere, and my paper slips off and slides across the room, landing right at Arjun's feet. All of it is so noisy that everyone's attention swivels to me. I curse under my breath.

"I'm sorry. I'm so sorry . . ." I say to everyone, my face, neck, and chest burning. They probably don't know I made this mess because I was essentially swooning, but I know, and I want to leave and hide in my cabin for eternity.

I set the easel right and gather my fallen materials, crawling on the floor on all fours. This is next-level embarrassing. The people next to me lean in to help, but I wave them off. I stick the pencils back on the drawing table tray and stand, brushing off my knees. In my peripheral I see someone standing in front of my station. My eyes lift to find Arjun holding my papers out to me.

"You dropped something." He grins at me.

Plucking the papers from his hands, I mouth the words "thank you" and sit. I expect him to go back to his seat, but he lingers for a moment.

"Are you okay?"

"I'm fine, yes. Go, go—sit back down." I wave him off and run my hands through my hair before straightening my things and waiting for my body temperature to come back down.

When I feel satisfied the room isn't staring at me anymore and I'm ready to get started, I pick up the pencil and put it to the paper. Immediately, I know it's wrong. I need a charcoal pencil for this, and if I know anything about being a creative it's not to ignore the call of whatever siren is singing.

I sneak out to the store and back into the studio as quietly as possible, not wanting to draw any more attention to myself. And this time, with the right tool in my hand and the memory of embarrassing myself ogling Arjun, I'm able to focus.

In one corner I test out a rough sketch of a full-body portrait of Arjun, but on a smaller scale. It doesn't feel quite right. But I glance between Arjun's face and my page again and something clicks.

My classes comes back to me faster than I expected, and in no time I have the outline of his face and body sketched. I lean back a little to take it in, figuring out where I need to go. I chew on my bottom lip, scrunching my brow. My gaze flicks between Arjun and the page, and I start to darken and solidify his shape. I work quickly, scrubbing away lines that aren't quite right with the pads of my fingers, smudging lines to get the shadows just right. I lose myself in the technique of it, bringing Arjun to life on my page.

But even after I've brought the basics to life there's still plenty of time left in the class. I sneak a peek at my neighbors' drawings, but they're not quite as far along as I am, so I study my sketch. Maybe I can add some detail somewhere, but model drawing is far from my expertise. Normally, I'd stop after getting this far, but I don't want to just walk out of the class.

I won't find what I need on the paper, though, so I zero in on Arjun again.

When I was in middle school, our art class took a field trip to the art museum. For most kids it was an opportunity to chat with their friends and cut up in a way they couldn't in class. For me it was like stepping into Narnia. It was the first time in my life I understood how art could capture emotion and tell a story. My teacher had to spend most of the day corralling unruly kids, but not me. She practically dragged me through the museum as I kept stopping to look at everything, until she saw me standing in front of Edvard Munch's "Melancholy" crying. Ms. Summer put her arm around me and said, "This is what art is about: expressing what it means to be human." I could feel the weight of the sadness in the painting. It was so heavy. I knew then I wanted to paint things that made people feel things too.

Technically speaking, my drawing isn't bad, but it won't make anyone feel anything.

Arjun's gaze moves around the room, and when it lands on me his face brightens with a smile. I fight a smile and look down at my drawing, biting my lower lip. How do I put that feeling on the page? The one where I feel my entire body melt when he looks at me. Or the one where my breath gets stuck in my chest and my muscles turn to goo.

I glance back up to see Arjun still staring. My cheeks heat, but I don't look away. And then I understand. It's his face—specifically, his eyes. No one has ever looked at me the way Arjun does, and this is what I need to put on the page.

I hunch back over the drawing, hoping time will stop, but it doesn't, so when Dany tells us two hours have passed, I feel the distinct weight of disappointment in my chest. I blink the fuzziness out of my eyes, stretching my aching body.

Dany finds her way over to me, eyebrows raised in question. I gesture to my piece of paper.

"Oh my gosh!" Her immediate excitement lifts the weight of my disappointment at not completely finishing. "Look! You're not blocked. Not fully anyway. You drew! And actually, this is really good, Mara." Dany leans in, studying my technique.

My stomach pinches and my mind races through every piece I've ever sold. Can she see M. North's style in my drawing?

She straightens, beaming, and hugs me. "I'm really excited for you. This means good things," she says, giving my shoulder a squeeze before moving on to talk to the other students.

I observe the drawing from Dany's perspective. She's right: it isn't bad, and even if it were, would it matter? I drew something. Nearly a full something. When I look up to compare my drawing to the model, Arjun is no longer in his chair. I find him in the crowd chatting with class participants, complimenting their sketches of him.

Something in my chest blooms, expanding out from my heart to every inch of my body. It's impossible not to be attracted to Arjun, but now I see it's equally impossible for me to deny the growing feelings I have for him.

He snakes through the small crowd making excuses and apologies while heading straight for me. My whole body feels like a garden in spring waking up from the winter's frost, flowers unfurling in the sun. When was the last time I felt like this?

"Can I see?" Arjun asks as he approaches, a shy smile on his face.

"Of course." I gesture for him to come to my side of the drawing table, and he does, standing close enough that if I swayed just a hair I could touch him. His woodsmoke and laundry detergent scent follows him like a gust of wind, wafting around me and drawing me in. "How'd I do?" I ask, observing his face for a reaction. I don't think he'd lie about liking it, but just in case.

"I didn't know I was this hot."

"Oh, stop." I nudge him with my elbow.

He sways away from me and then back, settling so close my entire body buzzes. "I'm kidding, but I'm also not. The eyes are. . . amazing." His voice is low and full of awe. "You're incredibly talented, Mara."

The way he says my name, I feel it in my bones the way you feel a beautiful note played on a cello. "Your turn," I say and hold out the piece of charcoal to him.

"Ha." He takes it from my hand and sets it on the easel tray, turning so he's facing me. He's so close I can't help myself—my eyes dart between his eyes and his lips. "How 'bout I make you dinner instead? At your place? I make a killer mac and cheese."

He looks at me, and for all I know, we're the only people in this room. Inside I'm dissolving, and I lean against the table, not trusting my knees to hold me up under the weight of his attention.

Even if I wanted to say no, I'm not sure I could.

11

I don't know how much time I have before Arjun will show up, so I run through the cabin like a tornado, picking up clothes and trash and generally just trying to make my place look less like the disaster it really is. I even have time to throw all my dishes in the dishwasher and scrub down the counters before Arjun knocks on the door.

I check my appearance in the big mirror on my dresser. My hair is in a thick, loose braid draped over my shoulder, a messy halo of thin hairs around my head. I try to comb them down, but it makes my hair look flat, so I tease it back to the messy look I had going before, except now it just looks too messy. I groan and rush to the door.

I saw Arjun a mere fifteen minutes ago, but as I open the door and take in his presence on my porch my stomach flutters as if I'm seeing him for the first time today.

"Hey," I say, a little out of breath.

"Hungry?" He holds up a reusable grocery bag bulging with goodies.

I nod and usher him inside.

After removing his boots, he walks into the kitchen as if it's his own, unloading the bag on the counter. He's brought four different blocks of cheese, a small container of milk, a bag of shell pasta, and a handheld cheese grater. I follow him into the kitchen, hovering nearby and leaning against the counter he's working on. He's every bit as graceful as he was the day we shared wine and cheese at the store. I think I could spend hours watching him do the simplest tasks and be every bit as mesmerized as I would be at some kind of magic show.

"You know, I want to make fun of you for bringing your own cheese grater, but I don't have one, so I'll applaud you for your foresight."

"I don't like to take any chances. I've had one too many cheese emergencies."

"What does a cheese emergency look like?"

"I don't want to give you nightmares. It's grim." His deadpan face has me fighting a smile.

"What are all these cheeses? I don't think I've ever had a mac and cheese that wasn't boxed."

Arjun leans back and grips his chest as if he's been shot, hands over his heart. His face is painted with mock pain. "You wound me, Mara."

"I'm sorry!" I bury my face in my hands.

"It's fine, it's fine. I'm just glad you're going to get the real experience tonight."

"Me too," I say and fold my arms across my chest. Having Arjun in my kitchen feels domestic and intimate, as if we've known each other for years and not just weeks.

"All right, so." He claps his hands and rubs them together. "We have Gouda, this guy is a five-year-aged cheddar, this one's Gruyère, and my crowning touch is Brie. It's a little radical, but I like to live dangerously." He points to each cheese as he names them. They're all varying shades of white and orange and assorted textures ranging from squishy to crumbly.

"No such thing as too much cheese, huh?"

"Never. Want to try them?" he asks.

"I thought you'd never ask. Let me get you a knife and cutting board." I move around Arjun to find the items, my shoulder brushing his back as I pass by. My body registers the contact, tingling in response.

I turn back to Arjun to hand him the tools, but he's already holding up a small chunk of cheese, right at mouth-level. The morsel sits between his forefinger and thumb. His hand is still, eyes fixed on mine. *Is he handing me this cheese or trying to feed it to me? Will it be weird if I let him feed me?* I lick my lips, looking back and forth between his fingers and eyes.

"Here, try," he says, moving the cheese toward me, our eyes locked on each other.

I lean forward, parting my lips. The cheese hits my tongue first, solid and salty. Then his fingers are against my tongue too, my lips. I use my tongue to claim the square of cheese, and as I close my lips they drag over his fingers, the earthy taste of them mingling with the cheese. My entire body heats and crackles. Under my skin small charges spark and pop. The air between us is so charged we could generate power.

"What do you think?" he asks, his voice low.

Does he mean the cheese or the part where his fingers were in my mouth?

"I . . . think I want more."

He's the first to break eye contact, taking the knife and cutting board from my hands, his lips pulled into a grin. He unwraps the other cheese blocks, slicing small pieces off the ends. "So the one you just tried was the cheddar. It's from a farmer south of Pueblo, Colorado. He ages his cheddar anywhere from three to ten years before selling it. This is a five-year-old cheddar, one of my favorites."

He's talking as if whatever just happened between us didn't happen. Did he not feel the palpable electricity between us? I'm having some trouble recovering. I dig my nails into my palms and focus on breathing steady breaths while Arjun points to the other cheeses, telling me about them and where they come from though I'm only half-focused on his words. I can't seem to take my eyes off his fingers, his hands, the little bit of forearm showing where his flannel sleeves are rolled up and I can see the way his muscle flexes as he moves. I know the way his skin tastes now—how am I supposed to pretend I don't?

I pick up a small morsel of each of the cheeses he points to and nibble on each one in turn, trying to act more normal than I feel. He starts to grate the Gouda, and I'm mesmerized by the way his biceps flex under his shirt. Staring at him for two hours in that art class has done nothing to minimize the desire I have to stare even more. To reach out and touch him, to—

"Mara?"

"Yes?" I blink a few times, meeting Arjun's eye.

"You were staring." The smirk on his face confirms I've been caught.

My face heats, and I straighten my shirt, brushing my hair back. "I was . . . um . . . the cheese looked really delicious, and I was just thinking that I'd . . ." I pinch some of the freshly grated Gouda and pop it in my mouth to avoid having to say any more. "Can I help you at all?" I offer, changing the subject.

"No way—this is my treat."

"Are you one of those people who doesn't like to share the kitchen?"

"If I am I blame the women in my life. If I had a dollar for every auntie who shooed me out of her kitchen I'd own a much bigger cheese shop."

"I like your cheese shop. I think it's the perfect size. Beer?" Anything to give me a second to recover from being caught staring at him. Spending twelve years with the same person has made me so rusty when it comes to dating.

"Yes, please. I like my shop too. I didn't really pin myself as a mountain town kind of guy, but I think I like it."

"Really? You definitely have a small-town mountain guy vibe. It's all that plaid, I guess."

"When in Rome."

Smiling, I pop the tops off two beers with a fridge magnet can opener. I slide one close to Arjun and stand at the end of the island, giving him enough space to move about the kitchen without me being underfoot. And to keep myself from reaching out to touch him.

"How did you end up here anyway? You were in France, for fuck's sake. Why come back to a tiny mountain town in the US?"

He takes a long drink of the beer, checking the label and nodding in approval. "France was great—I loved it there. But it never really felt like home. Colorado was always calling to me. And not just because my huge family lives here." Arjun picks up another cheese block, his entire upper body working to grate it. "I spent a lot of time in high school coming out to mountain towns for ski weekends with my cousins and some of our friends. My favorite part was always when we went out to eat at the end of the day. We'd end up in these little corner shops on some quaint Main Street with the best food.

Sandwiches you think about for months after you've eaten them, waiters who treat you like family, soups you try to replicate and never seem to get quite right. That's the shit that I came back for."

"Was that a dream of yours? Owning a quaint Main Street shop in a mountain town?"

"No, but that's because I was a dumb kid. I wanted to own a fancy restaurant in a big city like Denver. I wanted to be the chef they mentioned on the front page of the food section of the newspaper." Cheese grated, Arjun wipes his hands on a hand towel hanging on the dishwasher. "Pot for pasta?" he asks, and I point to the drawer under the stove. He retrieves it, filling it with water, sprinkling salt into the pot, and setting the stove dial on high.

While he waits he leans against the counter, picking up his beer. He seems content to cook for the two of us—something that leaves a familiar tang in the back of my throat. At the beginning of our relationship, Ben would cook for me and didn't seem to mind, but after a while he got sick of it and eventually stopped.

I make food for you and it goes cold because you won't stop painting for five fucking seconds. What a waste of my time. Cook your own fucking meals, lazy bitch.

I blink away the memory and take a drag on my beer. *Arjun isn't Ben, Mara.*

"Okay, so you go to culinary school to be a world-famous chef, but you fall in love with cheese," I say, prompting him to finish the story as I try to get Ben out of my head.

"But I fell in love with cheese, and when I graduated, I moved back home and worked in a deli for a couple years—but like a swanky boutique deli. Very Denver." He chuckles, and I smile, understanding. "And all the while, I was looking around for a place to make my own. But the city was so damn expensive, so I started hunting in the suburbs and my search kept expanding."

"All the way out here to Copper Springs."

"One weekend I'm out here, kind of by chance, and I see a restaurant with a for-sale sign. I kind of just wanted a space for a cheese shop, but I walked into Park's Deli and, man, it was like I was in high school again. That same feeling . . . I couldn't pass it up." Arjun beams, and I'm completely captivated by him. The way his skin crinkles around his eyes when he smiles, his self-assured movements in the kitchen, the way his eyes dance when he talks about his work. I could watch him cook and tell stories all day.

"I grew up going to Park's, and the Gouda Times Bistro is way cooler than Park's. I like what you've done with it."

"Thank you." He beams with pride. "It's hard to take over a place that's been a staple in the community, but everyone's been really welcoming."

"Do you feel like you're living your dream?"

"I think at sixteen I would have found this kinda lame. But thirty-three-year-old me loves it."

"Thirty-three? You told me you were an old man."

"Thirty-three is my cover age."

I smile into my beer bottle.

"I assume you're about the same age as I am?" he asks, opening up the pasta package and pouring it into the boiling water. He gives it a stir and finds a pan. "Can you get me a stick of butter and some flour?"

I set down my beer to retrieve the items. "Very close. I'll be thirty soon."

"Your birthday's coming up?"

"December fifteenth."

"Any special plans?" He heats the pan, setting the whole stick of butter in there.

Dinner by myself, staring at a blank canvas until inspiration strikes, crying over old photos...

"Nothing special."

"Hmm. Well, we'll see about that." He grins at me, turning back to the stove.

A warm feeling spreads all through me. My birthday is over six weeks away. He's talking about future plans, and not just next week future. It launches a thousand butterflies in my stomach and chest. I have to take a long, slow drink of my beer to come back down to earth again.

Arjun's focus shifts to the meal as things come together, so I grab a couple of bowls and forks, setting them on the counter. I also fill two glasses with water and lean on the counter again to watch him work.

"Did you like Dany's drawing class?" Arjun asks as he moves the skillet off the burner and turns off the stove.

"It was nice. It was way tamer than any art class I ever took."

"Tamer?"

"Yeah, um, usually the models for a full-body drawing class are nude."

Arjun makes a sound somewhere between a choke and a laugh while scooping generous portions of mac and cheese for each of us.

"The lady next to me seemed pretty excited at the prospect," I say. "She's probably just your type. Well, she's at least your age. In her seventies or so."

"I hope you gave her my number." Arjun wipes his hands on a dish towel and leans a hip against the counter, facing me. He's close enough to reach out and touch, and I inch my fingers along the counter toward his.

"I didn't know I was supposed to be your wingman tonight."

"I think I prefer you as my dinner date."

The look in his eyes makes it hard to think about anything except the urge to lean forward and kiss him. His skin brushes mine, our fingertips intertwining on the counter between us. My pulse soars.

"Do you always pick up chicks at art class?"

"Nah, I usually just show up at their houses with a 2008 Honda CRV and some homemade food. Gets 'em every time."

My cheeks hurt from smiling, and when he moves his hand away my fingers ache for his touch.

"Ready to eat?" he asks.

I nod, and he grabs the bowls of steamy mac and cheese before I lead him to the sunroom. The small table is covered in an assortment of random things: paint tubes, pages torn from sketchbooks, a plate, a half-empty cup, a pair of gloves. It's embarrassing, and I wish I'd remembered to clean this space. But Arjun doesn't make any comment, only helps me clear it.

The first bite sends me into another universe. I close my eyes, groaning at the absolute perfection. It's creamy and gooey, melting in my mouth. Layers of flavor slowly unravel in my mouth so that even after I've swallowed I'm still tasting new things.

I would swim in this mac and cheese.

"You like it?" Arjun asks.

Whatever noises I was making obviously got his attention. I nod enthusiastically, inhaling another forkful. "Incredible," I say around a full mouth of food.

His chest puffs a little at my compliment.

"I had no idea mac and cheese could be so good," I say.

"I aim to please," he says with a smirk that makes my stomach drop to my knees. I almost forgot how delicious it feels to flirt with someone. How it makes the world seem a different color. "Do you paint in here?" Arjun asks, gesturing to the room.

"When I paint, yes. And also when I stare at a blank canvas. The lighting is perfect for staring at things. But considering I haven't painted in nearly eight months this room isn't seeing much action. Except the staring. Plenty of that going on."

"But you drew tonight?"

"To my utter surprise, yes. But Dany thought maybe since it was a different medium I'd be able to, and she was right."

"Do you think it means you'll be able to paint again?"

"I don't know. I hope so. I miss painting."

Arjun reaches across the table holding his hand open in invitation. I place my hand in his, and he strokes his thumb across my knuckles.

"I wish I knew the right thing to say."

"It's okay that you don't."

He squeezes my hand, never looking away from me. His gaze is intense, his face painted with compassion. The sensation of his skin against mine is the only thing that exists in this moment, the way his thumb sweeps back and forth across my fingers. A meditation that soothes all my frayed edges.

My phone dings, pulling us both out of the moment. When his hand leaves mine there's a pang of disappointment in my chest. I look around for my phone, a little disoriented, eventually realizing the sound came from across the cabin and it's still in my jacket pocket.

"Why don't you check that, and I'll get started on cleaning the kitchen?" Arjun says, standing and collecting our bowls and silverware.

"I'll check it later. And you're the guest, so no way am I letting you clean up." I reach for the bowls, but he twists them out of my reach and heads into the kitchen.

"No way am I going to make a mess in your kitchen and not clean up after myself. You'd never invite me back."

"I think we both know that's not true. I'd slap my mother for more of that mac and cheese."

Arjun's laugh fills the cabin as I follow him to the kitchen. I load the dishwasher while he wraps the leftover cheese blocks in Saran Wrap. The whole moment is so domestic and serene, but my body is strung tight, like a cord that might snap at any minute. Even Arjun seems on edge, fumbling with the plastic wrap when he's normally calm and collected. When he's done packing his bag, he wipes the countertops, tidying everything on the counter as he does. I handwash the dishes, glancing back at him every so often. We do all this in a comfortable silence, the kind filled with anticipation of what might come next.

Kitchen cleared, Arjun takes his bag to the front door, pulling his jacket and boots back on. The clock reads 9 p.m., but the night feels young. I wish he'd stay longer. I don't have the courage to ask.

"Thank you for dinner. You weren't kidding about a killer mac and cheese."

"It was my pleasure." His smile launches my stomach on a wild ride, up into my throat and back down to my knees—which start to feel a little wobbly. He straightens, and for just a beat our eyes lock onto each other and time stops.

He's going to kiss me—I can see it in his eyes. Knowing this should make me more nervous than I am. He closes the gap between us, eyes darting between my eyes and lips. Maybe I shouldn't want it as much as I do, but my body doesn't know that. My hands ache with the need to touch him, and I reach out as he steps into my space, sliding my arms around his back. He's the kind of solid that would make me feel safe anywhere as long as he were nearby.

He holds me to him, this hug different than the one from earlier tonight. This one is charged, a cloud full of lightning waiting for the right moment to strike. His cheek is against my temple, and then his lips follow. I close my eyes, waiting for those lips to find mine and release the tension inside, but he pulls away.

"Thank you for a lovely evening," he says, meeting my eyes for the briefest of seconds before moving so quickly out of my arms and through the front door I barely have time to register what happened until I'm standing alone in my cabin.

What the hell?

Did I read that all wrong? Is what I'm feeling one-sided? I'm still trying to wrap my head around what just happened when there's a knock on my screen door and it creaks as it's opened.

I open the front door to Arjun, his hair mussed like he's been running his hands through it. "Arjun? Did you forget something?" I step back to give him space, but he closes the space between us instead.

His hands cup my face. If looks could devour, I wouldn't be standing here right now. As it is, I'm barely standing at all, my legs weak with desire. *Has any man ever looked at me like this?* I grip the fabric of his jacket, needing something to hold onto to steady me.

And then he leans in and touches his lips to mine. It is a kiss so sweet and tender tears form behind my closed eyes. It's the swell of the wave and the crashing relief of it. Phantom tastes of cheese and beer on my lips will haunt me for days.

When he breaks our kiss, he rests his forehead against mine, his hands moving down my neck and shoulders coming to rest on my arms. Our breath mingles in the space between us, both of us trying to catch our breath. I flatten my hands against his chest to see if his heart is beating as hard as mine, and when I feel the pound of it against my palm I know he's feeling everything I'm feeling too.

He pulls his head back, and our eyes meet. "That. I forgot that."

"Next time, don't leave without it."

"I won't," he says, kissing me again. And again and again and again.

And when he leaves, my fingers start to itch.

12

I practically jog to the sunroom, my impatient fingers tapping at my legs to move faster, go quicker. I was here just weeks ago, image burning in my brain, fingers itching to make a painting, and it was snatched away from me. But I have another chance and I don't want to lose it again.

Maybe last time I scared away inspiration with my desperation. Maybe I was too eager, so this time I'll stay calm, keep my cool. This time I'll speak quietly to her, assuring her I'm on her side, that we're a team and we can work together, but she has to stay. As I unwrap the plastic from the new canvas and set up the easel, I resist the urge to rush through the process, whispering pleas to my muse.

Just stay with me.

Making art has never been frantic for me; it's always been an endeavor rife with peace. I used to shut myself in my studio for entire days and keep the world out. Ben would bang on the door sometimes, threatening that if I didn't come out, he'd come in and drag me out himself. Usually I'd ignore him and he'd go away. To see Blair, as I found out later. For the most part he was all talk, but occasionally he'd storm in and start throwing my supplies around the room and bellowing at me.

"It's so fucking selfish how you spend your entire weekend in here with your stupid little hobby."

"My little hobby is our sole source of income."

"You have no sense of work-life balance. I've supported your ass for years because you won't get a real fucking job."

"And now I'm supporting yours."

I lost half my supplies that day.

The thing about spending so many years with someone is that remembering them is complicated. Because as often as Ben would barge in yelling toward the end of our relationship, it's hard to ignore all the years he'd come in with a hot meal, a bowl of ice cream, flowers, or a freshly made frame for me to stretch new canvas around. Sometimes he'd sit with me while I worked, doing his own work or reading. For as many moments of discord there were a hundred of peace.

Losing Ben was both heartbreak and relief. Losing the ability to paint has been unbearable.

So, nearly seven months later, large brush in hand, standing in front of this closed door poised to open it again, a wave of panic washes over me.

What if it disappears again?

What if I'm relegated to a life of almost being able to paint and never being able to follow through?

What if I'm always this broken?

That word snags on something in my brain.

Broken. Broken. Broken.

It weaves in and around the image in my mind: the face of a woman in pieces, not quite connected, not quite destroyed. The colors are muted, grayish pink and phthalo turquoise, raw dark sienna, and the darkest black I can find in my collection.

My pulse races in my throat, my stomach. Straining against every instinct to move faster, I take my time dipping the brush into the paint. It's luxurious, the feel of the brush in the liquid. Tears spring to my eyes unbidden at the beauty of this small moment, and when I drag my brush across the canvas, spilling color against the white, I let them flow freely.

Long after I've stopped crying, my vision blurs and I can't fully concentrate. I check the time to find it's somehow three o'clock in the morning. The image still hasn't left me and the painting is nearly finished. I don't know if it was just a fluke or if this is a permanent restoration, but whatever it is, I've got a painting in front of me that I painted myself and the sore back and arm muscles to prove it.

As I stand back to look at my art, goose bumps spread up my arms and down my back. A laugh bubbles out of my chest, and I step close to the canvas to inhale the scent of the acrylic paint deeply, drawing it into my lungs.

I did it. I painted again.

I've been waiting for this moment for months, and now it's here it feels even better than I imagined it would.

The summer after my freshman year of high school my parents took us on a cruise to the Caribbean. I packed a small bag of art supplies containing two notebooks, a pack of brand-new pastels, a watercolor palette, and brushes. I didn't realize until we were on the plane that I'd accidentally left it at home. I begged my mom for a piece of paper and a pen or pencil, of which she had neither, for something to do on the plane. To my utter embarrassment, she flagged down the flight attendant and asked for those things for her daughter. The look from that flight attendant had me swearing I'd never fly again on the off chance I ever ran into her, but she did as requested and brought me a piece of paper and pen. We didn't have time to stop into a supply store between getting off the flight and embarking on the ship, so I carried that ballpoint with me all week on the cruise, drawing on everything I could get my hands on. When I got back home, I practically kissed my art supplies, and for the next week I faked being sick so I could skip school and paint. My parents had to bring meals to my room so I'd eat.

I was a woman obsessed I had missed painting so much.

That feeling, the ache of reuniting with my art, floods me now, seeping into my joints and bones. I sit, heavy with the weight of reconciliation yet buoyed by the bliss of this moment. I hoped it would be filled with only joy, but as usual, I feel as many things as I have words for in my vocabulary and then some. They've been swirling all evening, but as I rest, they settle like dust in my soul, ready to be kicked up again the next time I paint.

I wake with a start, my phone screaming at me from somewhere nearby. Bleary-eyed and disoriented I hunt for it, only to miss the call by seconds. Jackie.

A text comes through immediately.

> Just wanted to see how things are going. Call me soon.
> *Kiss emoji*

I rub my eyes to clear the sleep from them. I stretch the crick in my neck, wincing at the soreness that will inevitably follow me all day. I'm too old to fall asleep on the couch, but I must have slept hard because it's ten in the morning. In a panic, I realize I fell asleep holding a paintbrush, but it isn't in my hand anymore. I find it half-stuck to the floor. I'm able to pry it up, and I stick it in a jar of water in case I can save it.

I close my eyes for just a moment, checking for the image, searching my soul for colors and ideas. They're all still there. The lightness I felt last night is still there too, and I touch my hand to my chest as if to try to keep it inside me.

Don't leave me again.

And it doesn't. It stays with me all day while I finish the painting, surviving off coffee and mac and cheese leftovers. I ignore my phone, dedicating my entire day to painting, and by the time I'm satisfied with it, the sun has started to set again and I have to turn on the lights to clean up the space properly.

When my sunroom is as organized as it's going to get and I can't contain my excitement any longer, I finally call Jackie back.

"Hey, stranger."

"Jackie. I have a surprise for you."

"I do love a surprise. But usually only the kind I know about beforehand."

I switch the call to a video chat, and Jackie's face appears on my screen. She looks put-together, her makeup perfectly done, eyebrows pristinely plucked and hair styled casually into a low ponytail, while I resemble a sickly Victorian poet, the bags under my eyes darker and more pronounced by the shadows in the room cast by my array of lamps.

"Are you hungover?" she asks.

"Be nice."

"That was nice."

I flip the camera screen to show Jackie my painting.

She gasps, her eyes go wide, her hand covers her mouth, and

she jerks, shaking the camera. "Oh my god. Oh my god, you painted! Mara!"

"I know," I say. I'm sure she can hear the smile in my voice.

"Holy shit, okay, can you get closer? Show me, like, the whole thing and then get close. Let me see all of it." She leans forward as if she'll see it better by getting closer to the phone.

I move toward the canvas, doing as she instructed, my stomach fluttering. Jackie is always the first to see my paintings. Since the beginning of our relationship she's seen them before anyone, including Ben. Of course, for a long time it pissed him off, but after a while he didn't care if he saw them at all, much less first. Jackie's stamp of approval means more to me than just the promise that my piece will sell, because Jackie isn't just an agent—she also has great taste. Her eye for art is unmatched among her peers. She's been on every "30 under 30" and "40 under 40" list for her rise in the ranks. Jackie knows good art, and even more than that, Jackie was the first one to see my art for what it could be.

For her to see me now would mean I haven't lost my touch. That even though I painted again, I didn't lose that thing that makes me *me*. That thing I've been missing since April. Hope swells in my chest.

"Wow, it's really different," Jackie says. She sounds surprised, but not in a bad way.

She's right: it is different from the stuff I've sold under my pseudonym. Different from anything she's seen before. Landscapes are my signature style, and Colorado is an artist's dream: forests, mountains, skies, and snowy roads. Until my grandparents died three years ago I'd come out here at least once a year by myself to breathe in the fresh mountain air, get inspired, and go home with fresh ideas. This isn't a landscape, though, or even anything close to it. It's an abstract portrait—something she's never seen me do.

What Jackie doesn't know is that I've painted things like this before. This morning when I woke up, I realized how similar this painting is to the ones hidden away in my storage shed.

"Step back again," Jackie says, the earlier excitement in her voice gone. She's got her agent hat on.

I move back so she can see the whole painting again. Her extended silence turns the excited fluttering in my stomach into a nervous fluttering.

"I can hear you thinking—you might as well do it out loud," I say.

"It's different."

"You mentioned that. Different bad?" I ask, the nervous fluttering turning violent, my insides practically shaking.

Jackie exhales through her teeth, clicking her tongue. "Not . . . bad."

"Jesus, Jackie, just say it." I flip the screen back around so she's looking at me instead of the painting.

"I support you." She pats her hand against her chest. "Let me start with that."

"I hate when you start with that." I sit on the couch rubbing my forehead. This is the opposite of how I wanted this call to go.

"I'm just nervous."

"As my agent or as my friend?"

"Both, maybe? This work is way deeper than your other stuff. Even if the girl in the painting isn't you, it's still very obvious how personal this is. And there's nothing wrong with that, but your other work doesn't have this vulnerability. Again, there's nothing wrong with that. None of that is bad. It's just different."

I chew on my bottom lip, waiting for her to go on.

"But you've been so consistent for the past decade that people expect that certain thing from M. North. And with a new sponsor, changing your style now may not be the best move."

"What's wrong with subverting expectations, Jackie? You watched *Game of Thrones*, didn't you?"

"You want this to be your *Game of Thrones* season eight? Did you enjoy that season?"

"No. It was garbage."

"Exactly. No one liked that."

So much for coping with humor. I run my free hand through my hair, grabbing it by the roots and exhaling a loud breath.

"Okay, so what are you suggesting? I can't just change my style—I paint what I paint. And for fuck's sake, this is the first painting I've done in close to eight months, Jackie. This is the first time I've created in over half a year and this is what came out. If the guy doesn't want to sponsor me as an artist no matter what my art is, then he can—"

"Okay, put down your pitchfork. I have a suggestion. You may not like it, but I'm going to suggest it anyway. What if we use this new work as a way to rebrand? And maybe for you to put these works out as yourself."

"Do you mean reveal M. North? Rebrand M. North as Mara West?"

"Yes." Jackie's lips pinch into a tight line. She fiddles with one of her earrings, waiting for me to respond.

My proverbial balloon pops. My insides shrinking, I droop against the couch. I was going to fight for this. I felt the walls come up, grabbed my guns from the armory . . . But now I just want to be done with this conversation. I called for support and now she's suggesting the last thing in the world I want to do.

"To be honest, Jackie, I can't think that far ahead right now." I drag my hand over my face. "I know you're always thinking of how to sell my work, and I love that about you, but what I needed from you today was support and only support. You know how hard this has been for me. I know the exhibition is around the corner, I know I usually have more done by now, but the fact I have this at all is monumental, and I thought you'd get that. That's why I called you. I wanted to celebrate this."

Jackie looks properly chastised. Her mouth twists and she squeezes her eyes shut, regret written all over her face. "You're right. I'm sorry." She covers her heart with a hand. "I should have come in today guns blazing, flag waving, running circles around you. So keep doing you, okay? Create whatever art you can, paint whatever you can paint. I'll worry about the sales and the exhibition and all of it. Don't think for one more minute about it. You just focus on making more beautiful pieces, and we'll go from there, okay?"

"Yeah, okay."

"Before I let you go, are you still good with the Denver show opening in two weeks? Do I need to cancel?"

I forgot all about it. Back in April, Jackie canceled all my exhibitions in the fall that required new work, but this one is a gallery showing private collection pieces. They don't require me to paint and both Jackie and I will get a small payout for it, so it's the only one I agreed to keep on the books.

"Yeah, that's fine. Are you flying out for it?" I ask.

"Are you attending? I will if you want to go. The gallery owner isn't expecting me or anything."

"I don't think I want to."

"That's settled then. I'll mail you the check when I get it."

Thank God. My bank account isn't looking so good.

We say our goodbyes, and I toss my phone on the floor.

Fuck.

Of course, Jackie's thinking of how my work will sell or not sell. Of how the world will look at it, how potential buyers will look at it. That's her job. Without this conversation I wouldn't have considered those things for a long time, but she's right: if I put this next to my old work, people might not believe they're made by the same artist.

I wonder if Dany can tell the difference.

But thinking of Dany now just brings back that pinch in my stomach. Dany, whose favorite artist is actually her friend lying to her. What happens when my exhibition comes around and I want to invite her but can't without revealing I've been hiding this Very Important Fact about me for months? As if it isn't bad enough I haven't told Dany, Arjun doesn't know yet either.

I run my fingertips over my lips, conjuring our kiss from last night. Was that just twenty-four hours ago? It feels like a lifetime since then. The pinching in my stomach intensifies. I can't keep this from him—not if we're . . .

Well, what are we?

God, this is a mess. I thought being able to paint again would fix everything. I thought once I got this back I'd feel like myself. Whole.

I thought I'd know who I am, but I still feel fractured.

My skin feels like my own and my soul feels like it's home again, so why do I still feel so lost?

13

*E*very time I have to mail a painting I kick myself for not choosing graphic design as a career path. No graphic artist ever had to wrap and lug canvases to the post office for their agent.

Despite the discouragement from Jackie about my first painting in nearly eight months, I haven't been knocked down completely. Within days I had another idea, something a little closer to my old style, a landscape—although this one's more abstract than real, so it doesn't match completely, but apparently the muses heard Jackie's concerns. I bought a big canvas for it, and I think it'll work as my commission for Gerhardt.

That first painting, "Girl in Pieces," took me about twelve hours. Record timing. The landscape took three weeks. Jackie asked me to mail them both as soon as I finished with this one. Fortunately, she's footing the postage bill.

The post office in town is still housed in the original building from the 1800s when Copper Springs was founded. They've added modern conveniences and it has the standard postal service flair, but the quaint exterior is as original as the beat-up wood floors—and the person behind the counter by the looks of it. The charm of Copper Springs is this exactly, the perfect blend of modern meets quaint and historical. It's the kind of place you fall in love with as a kid and then rekindle the romance as an adult. I always said I wanted to live here growing up, and now that I am grown-up it's exactly as great as I thought it'd be.

I hand off my paintings, happy to be free of them, the weight of the exhibition immediately a little lighter. Next week is Thanksgiving, and that gives me three full months to knock out eight paintings. It's not ideal, but the pressure doesn't feel so intense.

It's a stunning November day. Cold but the sun is shining, and as I walk toward my car I pause to soak it in. Things are looking up. I'm painting again, I've got a new friend, and things with Arjun are . . . well, I don't know what they are, but they're good. Things are better than they've been all year in fact—maybe better than they've been in many years.

For once, my empty cabin doesn't hold the same appeal as it usually does. I haven't had lunch yet, and the bistro sounds like exactly the place I want to be right now. I stop by The Artist's Outlet first to see if Dany wants to join me, but it's closed.

Weird. Maybe she's in the studio.

> Stopped by the store to see if you wanted a late lunch.
> Are you around?

At the bistro, come hang!

. . .

When I arrive at the bistro I pause in the doorway, surprised at the transformation. All the small tables are gone, replaced with taller tables that wouldn't look out of place at a wedding or cocktail hour. Each of them has a black tablecloth crumpled on top of it waiting to be arranged. The counter where customers normally give their orders or sit while waiting for a cappuccino is in disarray, stacked with various wines and cheeses, and the place is strangely absent of food smells. Instead, Pine-Sol and wine hit my nose as I walk in.

"Hey!" Dany yells across the bistro. She waves and gestures for me to join her over at the counter she's standing behind.

Arjun, two young boys wearing black aprons, and a guy I recognize from the kitchen staff all turn to look at me. Everyone blinks and goes back to their tasks. That is everyone except Arjun.

"Mara? What are you doing here?" A slow smile creeps across his face.

"I was hungry. I was just at the post office and thought I'd come get some lunch, but I see I've come at a bad time."

"No, no, no." He gives the two boys the "one minute" finger and makes a beeline for me, crushing me against him. We just saw each other a few days ago for dinner at his place, but he hugs me as if it's been months. "Let me make you something to eat." He takes my hand and leads me to the counter, gesturing for me to sit on a stool.

The countertop is cluttered with jars, cracker boxes, various blocks of cheese, bags of deli meat, rolls of summer sausage, and piles of utensils, napkins, and small plates to complete the chaos.

"What's all this?" I ask, but Arjun disappears into the kitchen.

"This counter is going to be a giant charcuterie board," Dany says as she sorts items into categories. "It's for the cheese-and-wine event. You forgot about it, didn't you?"

It must be written all over my face. Forgetting about events is a regular occurrence for me when I'm sucked into a project. Ben never missed a chance to berate me for it, but Dany just cackles.

"To be fair, it was for a good reason," I say.

She raises her eyebrows at me.

"I was painting," I elaborate.

Dany's face transforms. Gone is the joking twinkle; her jaw practically unhinges as she runs around the counter to tackle me in a hug, making me lose my balance on the stool. "Mara, I am so, so happy for you," she says.

I hug her back, relishing in her celebration.

"What's all this?" Arjun asks, reemerging from the kitchen.

Dany skips back to the other side of the counter as he sets a sandwich on a plate in front of me. "Mara's painting again," she says, beaming like a proud mom.

Arjun smiles too, but the smile doesn't reach his eyes. "She is," he says.

"Oh, you already knew. Am I the last to know?" Dany asks, pouting.

"Best for last," I say. When Arjun starts to walk away, I tug on his shirt. "Thanks for my sandwich. You didn't have to do that."

He plants a kiss on my forehead. "I wanted to. I gotta get back to it, but stay as long as you like, Mara. I hope you're still coming tonight."

I nod, my mouth full of food, and he disappears into the kitchen again, snapping at the two boys who've apparently just been standing nearby. They startle into action, grabbing blocks of cheese and taking them over to a cutting board where they start to chop up the blocks, bringing the cut cheese back over to the counter to be arranged.

"He seems kinda stressed," I say.

Dany shrugs. "Yeah. He likes hosting, but not really the detail work. He likes the part where he gets to talk to people. That's why I started doing this. Arjun can arrange a mean charcuterie, but a big one like this on top of everything else? It's just a lot."

I nod in understanding. "Can I help?" I ask. While I've been eating Dany's started to arrange crackers on a giant piece of wood I didn't notice before. It looks like massive cutting board, the sort normally found with this kind of spread.

"Yes, please. This always takes me forever."

"So how did this event get started?" I ask as she trades me a pair of latex gloves for my empty plate.

"You'll have to ask Arjun for the full story, but from what I know, it kind of just seemed like a fun way to gather with the community at first. But then it became so popular Arjun was getting in trouble with the fire marshal, so he needed to find a way to cap the number of people who came."

"Jeez."

"Yeah, so he made it a ticketed event and all the money goes to support a local rescue farm that takes in animals with extra needs. It's such a cool place—you should go sometime."

"That's pretty amazing."

"And people keep showing up. They love it. I mean, who doesn't love a cheese-and-wine event? But they love Arjun really. The whole community does," Dany says.

Of course the community loves him. He's deeply lovable, although the "L" word makes my stomach feel like a bee colony.

It takes us almost an hour to arrange the counter, and then I follow Dany around the bistro to help with the rest of the setup:

wineglasses, signs, and backup food prearranged for the waiter who'll be manning the counter. We work right up until the start time, putting final touches out right as the first group of people walk in and the music goes on.

Arjun is the first one to greet everyone as they arrive, personally checking their reservations. His shoulders are tight, and I can see the muscles in his jaw working. When there's a lull in the check-ins, I sneak across the room and slide up next to him.

"Are you okay?" I ask, my voice low.

He nods, but his eyes are dim and tired. "Yeah, just a little—ya know. These nights are always kinda crazy for me."

"I'm here to help, so why don't you give me something to do?" I take his hand in mine, caressing the back of it with my thumb.

"Seriously, it's fine. Go get yourself a glass of wine and enjoy the event."

"Arjun." I maneuver my head to catch his gaze, which darts all around the room. When I squeeze his fingers he finally looks at me. "You don't have to do this all by yourself, and just because you want to doesn't mean you can. And just because you can doesn't mean you should."

He sighs. It's the sound of letting go, but also of being annoyed I so accurately called him out. "Can you make sure Zane and Bobby are doing the wines right? Zane has whites and Bobby has reds, but they don't know their heads from their asses and they should only be pouring an inch or so in every glass. When I told them how much to pour, Zane said—and I quote—'Oh, like beer pong.' How do sixteen-year-olds know about beer pong? I didn't do that till I was in college."

"Anything else?" I ask, trying to contain my smile, but I don't do a great job.

"And then if you could just check with the owner of the farm

—her name is Sherry; she's in the denim jumpsuit with the pigtail buns—to ask if she got my check from last quarter and tell her not to leave tonight before I—" He stops talking as people walk through the door, releasing me without a second thought, and I wander away to do as he asked.

I find Sherry first, passing on the message and what was probably the rest of Arjun's thought train, and then find the boys. Zane and Bobby are doing just fine, as I suspected. They look nervous, but they're pouring perfectly and everyone seems happy as they walk away. Maybe they were onto something with the beer bong.

I give Arjun a thumbs-up from across the room and grab my own glass of wine to wander around in search of a familiar face. Everyone seems in good spirits, some people reuniting, others obviously on a first date or out by themselves looking for someone to talk to. Eventually, I spot Ethel. She's by herself, twirling a wineglass and watching the room with an observer's eye. I have a feeling she sees more than she says.

"Fancy seeing you here," I say, setting my plate of cheese and the glass on the table.

"Well, I'll be damned. It's my drawing-class neighbor."

I give a silly curtsy, and Ethel bows.

"How did your drawing turn out?" I ask, realizing I never saw the end result.

"Oh, it was garbage. They always are, but I love it so much I don't care."

"I like your attitude. I wish I cared a little less."

"It comes with age. You lose all kinds of shit as you get older—your vision, your hearing, all the fucks you used to give."

I snort.

"I saw your drawing. You're pretty damn good." Ethel steals a slice of cheese from my plate. I nudge it toward her so she knows I don't mind, though I don't think she was worried about that.

"I hope so. It's how I make a living." *Even if right now I'm not making a dime.*

"Do you make comics or something?"

This elicits a bark of a laughter from me. "No, no. I'm sorry, I don't mean to laugh so hard. I paint and sell my paintings."

"Well, I'll be damned." Ethel takes a large sip of her wine. "I'd love to see your work if you've got any pictures."

I hesitate. Yet another opportunity to be honest and tell someone the truth of who I am. Someone I'm not romantically involved with or actively hiding my identity from while building a friendship. Someone I could tell without the guilt of already having lied about it. But as I pull out my phone and scroll through my photos, that icy-cold feeling overcomes me and I know I can't. I'm just not there yet.

"Nothing on my phone." I click it off and stuff it back in my pocket. "But I'll show you some day."

Ethel nods in approval and takes an olive from the plate, popping it into her mouth. There's a lull, the kind that stretches between two near strangers as they attempt to navigate a conversation.

"Any Thanksgiving plans, Ethel?"

With Thanksgiving only a week away, it seems like a natural question even if I don't really like to think about the holiday. Between the anniversary of my grandparents' deaths and the blowup with Charleigh, this is a painful time of year for me.

"My sister will drive down from Casper, and we'll make a nice meal for two."

"Wyoming? Wow. That's a bit of a hike."

"We don't mind it—we're making up for lost time."

"What do you mean?"

I love knowing the deepest parts of people, but it occurs to me when Ethel takes a long pull on her wine, draining the glass, that maybe not everyone likes to open the door to their darkness right away and she might be one of those people. I'm about to apologize for being too nosy when she sighs.

"I'm gonna need more wine to tell the whole story, but I'll tell you this: we had a falling-out about twenty years ago. My husband died five years ago from a heart attack—killed him so quick I didn't get to say goodbye. I got a new perspective on life that day, on what really mattered. I called my sister the day after he died, and we've been trying to make up for those fifteen years ever since. Been trying to convince her to move down here to live with me, actually, but she's stubborn as a mule."

My heart squeezes, both for Ethel's story and the reminder of my own falling-out with Charleigh. We're repairing, but I've been slow on the uptake, hesitant out of my own embarrassment at the situation.

"Is she an older sister? Younger?" I ask.

"She's my twin. My husband would always get onto me about it. 'You'd better forgive that damn twin of yours. You ain't right when you ain't right with her.' And then Gary left the world so fast, and I didn't want to live with any regrets." Ethel's eyes gloss with tears. She sniffs hard, clearing her throat. "Anyway. Pearl and I are right as rain now." She nabs another cheese slice from my plate. "You got a look on your face. You must have a sister."

"I do. Older sister. And we . . . had a thing too." The lump in my throat keeps me from saying more. I want to share, especially after Ethel's been open with me. I want to tell her everything, but even with a wide-open door I can't seem to find the words. I take a drink of my wine, hoping it will clear the dry feeling in my throat.

Ethel waits for me to continue, picking at the nuts on my plate.

"But it was my fault," I say.

"You gonna fix it?" Ethel fixes me with a gaze that would intimidate a dictator. *I bet she was a great lawyer.* But even under that steely gaze is a softness. She must get the sense this is hard for me and is giving me an out from explaining it all. So I take it.

"I'm trying."

"Good. Now what do you say we fill these glasses again?"

I offer to refill them, and after I return Ethel's to her Arjun flags me down to ask if I can give the waiter behind the counter a hand refilling the goodies. Happy to help, I do exactly as requested, and when I finish I find myself bustling about with the other staff, tidying empty glasses, chatting with guests as they leave, and at the end of the night counting donations and putting the diner back together.

As I'm walking to the door, tired in the best kind of way and ready to crash, a familiar hand catches my own, stopping me in my tracks. Arjun, worn down and glistening with sweat, smiles at me. It's not his full thousand-watt smile, but it still makes my knees a little weak.

"There's a Christmas tree lighting the Sunday after Thanksgiving. Would you be interested in going with me? As my date."

The whole moment is reminiscent of another local festival Arjun asked me to. I feel warm all over and buzzy. Maybe it's the alcohol. Maybe it's the way this man looks at me.

"Of course." I go up on my tiptoes to plant a quick kiss on his lips.

He promises to text me the details, and I push into the cold night air to walk back to my car.

While I wait for my windshield to defrost and the car to warm up, Ethel's words clang around in my head. I take a deep breath, pull out my phone, and click on Charleigh's name.

"Hey, you okay? It's late."

"I'm sorry," I say.

"For what?" She sounds genuinely confused.

"Three years ago. Thanksgiving, after the funeral, when you confronted me and told me what I needed to hear. You were right. And I knew you were right and I hated it. I'm sorry. I'm sorry I kicked you out of my life. I'm sorry I wasted three years of our lives not speaking to you."

When I was young, I once saw a magician pull a string of connected scarves out of his mouth. I spent years believing he really did pull those colorful cloths from inside him. I remember thinking what a relief it must have been to get all that cloth out—he must have been holding it in the whole show. Of course, I learned later it was just a trick. But now, having said the words that have lived inside of me for years, I feel like that magician. An endless stream of colorful scarves finally pulled out from where they've been knotted and tangled up inside.

"Oh, Mara." Charleigh's voice is tender, and I can hear the swell of tears in her voice.

"I know you probably forgave me ages ago, because that's who you are and how good you are, but you deserved this apology," I say, and I hear her sniff.

"I did. I forgave you immediately."

I squeeze my eyes, tears finding their way out anyway. "I missed you so much those years," I say, my voice a whisper.

"I missed you too, Mars Bar."

"But no more? Can we be us again?" I ask.

"Let's be us again."

14

I want to look cute for the Christmas tree lighting and my first official date with Arjun, but I also want to be warm, and the number of items in my wardrobe that hit both categories is limited. I settle on jeans, my snow boots, a long-sleeve thermal T-shirt, and a sweater under a long peacoat. I curl my hair and make sure it still looks cute after putting on a beanie, then I throw on some mascara and eyeliner even though it will mostly be dark. I study myself in the full-length mirror. I look Colorado cute. Maybe even just regular cute. I snap a photo of my outfit and text it to Dany.

* * *

How's my outfit? Okay for a first date?

I'D DATE YOU. Jk. Gorgeous!!!
　Arjun will be like *drool emoji*

. . .

Dany's texts lift my spirits, but only for a moment. I pace the cabin flapping my hands to rid the nerves, taking deep, exaggerated breaths. I don't even know why I'm so nervous—this is just like Fall Fest, and we've already kissed. We both like each other. We've been seeing each other casually for a few weeks.

It's just a date.

But it's basically my first "first date" ever. Ben and I didn't really date. We sort of fell into bed and eventually decided to be exclusive. And I definitely don't count any high-school dates. Making out in the back of a movie theater and getting fries and a milkshake at a diner afterward is hardly a date—it's just what high schoolers do.

I press my hands against my fluttering stomach, breathing in through my nose and out through my mouth so I don't lose my lunch. Maybe I'm not ready for this. I should text him and cancel. I'll just tell him I'm not feeling well, which isn't strictly a lie since my stomach is in knots.

But as I'm composing the text message there's a knock at my door. *Too late now.* I stuff my phone back in my pocket and wipe my sweaty palms on my jacket. I haven't seen him since the cheese-and-wine event last week, and when open the door to a smiling Arjun my stomach soars into my throat.

His hair is styled and combed back and to the side, and he's dressed warmly but not as casual as usual. He looks like a man who just walked off the cover of a magazine. Instead of a puff jacket he's wearing a navy peacoat, a plaid scarf tucked into the top. A gray sweater peeks out from the coat at his wrists, and I catch a whiff of cologne as the wind kicks a breeze toward me. His smile is the crown of his outfit, though, making my heart race in a way that tells me what I might not have been fully ready to admit before: I've got it bad for this guy.

145

"Hi," I say, unable to control the smile that takes over my whole face.

"You look . . ." He gives me a once-over, eyes trailing the length of my body.

"Like I made a little effort?" I lock the door and join him on the porch.

"Stunning." He tugs on my jacket, and my feet obey, our bodies drawn together like magnets. "Did you dress up for me?" he asks, his mouth inches away from mine.

All my nerves from earlier dissolve this close to him. I glide my hands down his arms, drinking him in. "Yes."

"Lucky me," he says, brushing his lips against mine in the softest kiss, and I consider cancelling for other reasons. But then he takes my hand and leads me to the car.

I shove away the disappointment that pinches me. *There's always later.*

"Milady," he says as he opens the door to his Subaru.

I slide into the passenger seat of the already warm car. "What's this?" I ask, pointing to two thermoses in the cupholder as he settles into the driver's seat.

He turns on the seat heaters, a sneaky smile on this face. "Mulled wine."

When I lift the lid of one of the thermoses steam rises, filling the car with the scent of red wine, cinnamon, and orange. "Did you make this?"

"Would you be impressed if I said yes?"

"I'll have to do a quality check first," I say with a smirk.

"By all means."

He backs out of the driveway, and I take a tiny sip. It tastes exactly the way it smells: sweet, spicy, and a little tart. The alcohol burns on the way down, flavors dancing on my tongue long after the liquid is gone. An uninhibited groan escapes my mouth.

He chuckles. "I'm going to take that as a yes."

* * *

The ride is short, and Arjun parks in the same place we did for Fall Fest. We walk to the park, where a large unlit Christmas tree awaits its chance to shine. Next to the tree a choir sings Christmas carols accompanied by a quartet. The area in front of them is empty, save for the families chatting and children chasing each other, no one gathered for the lighting yet as the sun hasn't fully set. Lines of people wait in front of food trucks selling hot ciders, regular and spiked hot chocolates, waffles and ice cream, and mini burgers and fries. Between the smells and sounds and the light dusting of snow it feels exactly the way a Christmas tree lighting should, full of the magic and hope of the holiday season.

"I thought we could take a quick tour of the food trucks before the tree lighting."

"Is this going to be like Fall Fest except everything's peppermint-flavored instead of pumpkin?"

"Nope. Even I draw the line somewhere, and peppermint cotton candy is that line."

"It's nice to see you have some standards for food."

"Some might say I have the highest standards."

"Says the guy who sells cheese for a living."

"Hey now, cheese is a gourmet culinary experience appreciated only on the highest levels by world-class gastronomists," Arjun says with a dramatic flair, gesturing to emphasize the important words.

"Says the guy who *sells cheese* for a living," I repeat, slowing down my words.

Arjun nudges me with his elbow, and I catch his arm, looping my hand around it. He squeezes my hand against his side and grins down at me.

The food trucks vary in size and color, exquisite smells wafting from them to me. Fried dough covered in cinnamon sugar, homemade chocolate candies, hand pies filled with savory meat and veggies, apple strudel, and any number of things I can't identify. People walk by with their mugs of mulled wine made by one of the food trucks, but I don't have to try it to know Arjun's homemade version tastes way better.

"I want to know more about your art career," he says as we amble through the crowd.

My stomach pinches. Of course he does—that's what you talk about when you're getting to know someone. *This is when you tell him, Mara. This is when you come clean.*

"What do you wanna know?"

"Well, do you sell a lot of art?"

"At the moment, not much."

"But you're painting again, right?"

"Yes, but this is for an exhibition, so they won't sell until the opening in March. If they sell at all, of course." It doesn't matter how many times I put my art out into the world, I'm always worried no one will connect with it. Maybe they'll buy it, maybe they won't, but what I want is for people to connect. Although my bank account hopes they'll buy it too.

"An exhibition? Wow. I'm assuming this isn't your first one."

I chuckle, but there's a nervous edge to it. I wish I had the courage to just tell him. A lie by omission is still a lie, and if this kissing and flirting is headed where I think it is, where I hope it is, I'm going to need to be honest, and soon.

But not tonight. I won't ruin tonight. I want it to be perfect.

"No, not my first exhibition. But the first one I'm unprepared for. This one is a big deal—there's a lot riding on it, more than any other exhibition I've done. I only have two paintings, and I need ten. It's the first time I've choked under pressure."

We've wandered to the end of the food trucks where the crowd has thinned out, and Arjun must sense my anxiety about it all because he stops, turning me to face him. His free hand slides down my arm, comforting and tender. A swirl of emotions kicks up in me—worry, fear, shame—and my throat feels tight.

"This is not you choking. You deserve more credit than you're giving yourself. You didn't paint for—how long was it?"

"Seven months."

"Seven months. And you're painting again, but you're just getting your feet under you. That's a sputtering engine coming to life. Not a dying one."

Shrugging, I mutter a vague agreement, my eyes fixed on the ground.

He puts a finger under my chin, lifting my face so our eyes meet. "You should be proud of yourself," he says.

I nod with some conviction, letting his words seep into my soul. It hasn't felt like anything to be proud of, but the way he looks at me, the way he encourages me makes me want to be proud of myself. He offers me his elbow, so I loop my hand through his arm again, and we walk back toward the tree.

"I thought your cheese-and-wine night was really successful. That's a great event you put on," I say.

"Yeah, they're always great. They've just gotten so big, and events aren't really my thing. I mean, I like the people. Just . . . details and stuff." A look of disappointment passes over his face.

"Why keep doing them if they're so stressful?"

"The community loves them. I started as a way of connecting with people when I took over Park's. I wanted people to like me." He shrugs, his voice a little too quiet, and chews on his bottom lip. "Especially in those early months. I was dealing with Roshni and the redesign, and the store wasn't doing great. I feel like I need to make it up to the community."

"From what I can see, you're well-loved in the community." I squeeze his arm. "And maybe it's because you earned their love by going over and above. Or maybe they just like you for you. And your cheese for being so delicious." I tilt my gaze up to his with a grin, but his brows knit together like maybe he doesn't believe me. I can taste his doubt, his insecurity—it's a metallic tang at the back of my throat. I recognize it. The life of an artist is filled with this stuff.

"Maybe," he says as we approach the main crowd again.

I give his arm another squeeze and lean my head against his shoulder. I don't always have the right words, but I want him to know I'm here, that I care. He hugs my arm to his side and plants a quick kiss on my forehead.

Arjun and I follow the throng of people to the empty space in front of the tree where the choir is finishing up their last song. The crowd's quieter near the singers, their songs filling the park in perfect harmony. Their voices float around us, wrapping us in the spirit of Christmas. Arjun stands behind me, one of his hands resting on my upper arm. I lean into his touch, closing my eyes to soak in this moment, this evening. I haven't felt this kind of connection with someone in so long. What I had with Ben was passionate and primal and somehow never as authentic as what I've shared with Arjun in the span of one evening.

When the choir finishes their song and the conductor steps away from the portable music stand, the sound of conversation rises into the silence, a brief and awkward transitional moment punctuated by the squeal of a microphone. A hush falls over the crowd. Then a woman not much older than me steps up to the mic.

"Who is that?" I whisper, leaning into Arjun.

"City councilmember Kelly Ghujar."

"Welcome, Copper Springs, to our thirteenth annual Christmas tree lighting! I hope you all have had a fun evening. Isn't the choir lovely? Let's give them a round of applause."

The sound of gloved clapping echoes into the night.

"This year our choir and quartet come to us from Trinity Lutheran—thank you so much, guys. You've really made this year a special one." She gives them a thumbs-up, and the choir members all smile back at her, pleased with the validation. "Without any further ado, the moment you've been waiting for: let's get a countdown going! Ten . . . nine . . . eight . . ." She turns to face the tree, her voice fading out as the crowd picks up the counting.

"Seven . . . six . . . five . . ."

Arjun's chest vibrates against my back, his voice louder in my ears than all the others.

"Four . . . three . . ."

His hand skims down my arm and he slips his gloved hand into mine, interlacing our fingers as best we can. A chill dances up my spine, but not from the cold.

"Two . . . one."

All at once the tree lights up—bright, colorful lights against the dark needles, illuminating the night. Children gasp and point, a few people whoop and shout, and everyone claps. The quartet and choir start up with a slow rendition of "O Christmas Tree."

I tip my head up and back to look at Arjun, soaking in all the childlike wonder of this moment. "Lovely."

His face is inches from mine. "Lovely," he echoes back to me, but I don't think he means the tree.

I lick my lips, my eyes darting between his his eyes and lips, which are so close to mine. The crowd fades away, the whole world a blurry background to us standing here, his hand in mine, lips so close. When we finally kiss it only lasts a second, but it awakens something in me that's been dormant for a long time. It sends a spark from our lips to my knees and back up, settling low in my abdomen.

"What'd you think?" he asks.

"Much more exciting than when my dad would light the tree."

Arjun laughs, nodding in a way that tells me he probably had a similar experience as a kid. "Did you want anything to eat?" he asks.

"I think I'm ready to go home. Plus, I'm out of wine and my toes are getting cold."

It's not a lie—I am cold, but mostly I'm ready to get out of here and get back to my cabin with Arjun.

On the car ride back Arjun rests his hand on my thigh. We steal surreptitious glances at each other, my stomach rioting, but not with nerves. He parks in front of my house, and we both sit in the car for a minute.

Arjun is a gentleman, and I know he won't come in unless I invite him. But I plan to.

When I lean across the middle seat he meets me halfway, our lips colliding in a kiss that starts chaste. But then his hand slides to the back of my neck, where he presses his fingers to deepen our kiss, and as his tongue finds mine a fire in me roars to life. I curl my fingers in and through his hair, gripping, needing to be closer to him. I try to adjust, but in my haste I move in such a way that the console jabs me. Clutching at my ribs I groan in pain, killing the moment.

"Oh, shit. Are you okay?" he asks, placing a hand over mine on my ribs. The worried look on his face is so sweet I just want to kiss him again.

"Yeah, just haven't made out in the car in a long time. I'm a little rusty."

His eyes are already alive with the pleasure I feel in my own body, but when he smiles at my joke it cracks something open in me. God, am I hungry for this man.

"Come inside," I murmur as I inch closer to him again, stretching over the console. Light as a feather, I touch his lips with my own and then tilt my head, repeating the soft brush of my lips on his neck, just under his jawline.

There's a sharp intake of breath and the movement of his jaw telling me he's nodding. Before I can kiss him again his door is open and he's advancing to my side of the car to open mine too. The air smells like snow and the only sounds are of our feet crunching on the gravel, the distant calls of nocturnal creatures, my blood rushing through my ears, and then the silence of my cabin.

I should add wood to the stove and warm the place up, but if it's cold I can't feel it. Arjun wastes no time in removing my hat and unbuttoning my jacket, peeling it off and hanging it up, kissing me in between each article of clothing as if he can't help himself. He takes off his own jacket next, and I unwind the scarf from around his neck, hanging everything carefully on the pegs. He kneels down, only looking away to unlace and remove his boots, but the absence of his hands and lips on me just aggravates the ache that builds inside.

I clench my fists, nails digging into my palms, as he sets his shoes aside and starts to unlace mine next, his slow, intentional movements creating a frustrating internal frenzy. Arjun glances up at me, his gaze capable of melting ice. The sight of him kneeling before me sends a throb of desire through a part of me that's long been neglected. He starts to stand, hands traveling up my calves, over the backs of my thighs, and as he stretches to his full height he tightens his grip on me, fingers digging into that place just under my butt to lift me up. Surprised, I let out a small yelp and wrap my arms around his neck, locking my legs around his waist.

"I wasn't expecting that," I say.

"I'm full of surprises," he rasps, and his grin is so unbelievably sexy I can't stop myself from leaning in to take his lips with mine, to claim that smile for myself.

He takes two steps forward, lips locked, and presses my back against the front door, his body hard against me. Even through my layers I can feel every contour—all the solid places, all the parts of him that want me. His hands are no exception; they creep under my shirt, branding me, staking territory.

Polite as Arjun is, he's greedy now, taking without asking, although the answer would have been yes anyway. He must know given the noises I make as his kisses trail lower, down my neck to my collarbone, where his tongue meets the sensitive skin there.

He pins me to the door with his hips and in one swift motion removes my sweater and the shirt I had underneath it. I hiss when my hot skin touches the cold door, and without a word Arjun wraps both arms securely around me and takes me to my bedroom.

He lays me on the edge of the bed as if I'm made of glass. I only release him from my legs when he stands and removes his shirt. I sit up, eyes level with his abdomen, which isn't all hard edges and defined lines; there's a softness to him, and I explore every inch of his exposed skin with my hands, my mouth. He runs his fingers through my hair, and when I unbutton his jeans his breath hitches. I'm ravenous for more—more of that sound, more of Arjun slowly unraveling.

I try to take more, but he leans toward me, boxing me in with his arms, and lowers himself over me, pressing me into the mattress. He dips his head, kissing my neck as I squirm underneath him. He must know what he's doing to me.

"I want you. I want all of you," he says, his breath warm on my neck, hands roaming my body.

"I'm yours."

His hands and mouth eventually find me—all of my untouched, neglected parts—and he breathes life back into them. I'd forgotten how it felt to be lit on fire from the inside. To be wanted wholly and completely. How healing it is to be desired and claimed. But Arjun has woken me up, stirring me from a dark, lonely slumber. Maybe he means he just wants all of my body; maybe he means he wants me body, soul, and spirit.

Whatever he wants I'm his for the taking, and whatever he means he takes me at my word.

15

"*D*on't you have to work?" I ask the wall of balloons standing on my porch. Arjun is buried beneath them, having promised to come early and help cook, but he's way earlier than I expected since he told me he'd be at a farm visit most of the afternoon.

"The farm visit was an excuse to surprise you. It's your birthday. I'm not working on my girlfriend's birthday." He walks in, bags in one hand and balloons in the other, releasing them so they scatter across my cabin and float up to the ceiling. He drops the bags and hooks his fingers in the loops of my jeans, tugging me closer.

"Girlfriend, huh?" I ask, threading my fingers through his hair.

"It was less syllables than 'the beautiful girl I'm sleeping with.'" He plants a trail of soft kisses along my neck.

"Girlfriend sounds good to me," I say.

"Good," he says, his breath warm on my neck. It's distracting as hell. But I have people coming over, and I have to focus.

My birthday dinner is being hosted here tonight, and even though I've spent the morning scrubbing both bathrooms, vacuuming all the dust in the cabin, and prepping to mop, the kitchen still hasn't been touched and the sunroom needs to be tidied. Cleaning on your birthday should be illegal, but who has time to clean when there's a handsome cheesemonger to kiss?

"You know you don't have to sweet talk me if you want to help clean. I'll let you do that for free."

"And if I just came to distract you with your birthday present. . .?" he murmurs, his hands sliding up the edges of my shirt, tickling my sides.

I grab his wrists to keep his hands from going any farther. As much as I want to let him continue, if we get started I won't want to stop. "Then you're getting kicked out until later today cause I've got a house to clean."

"Okay, okay. You win. Well, cleaning wins. And that's a loss for all of us."

Arjun's been in my kitchen a lot over the past two weeks, but watching him now I'm struck by how natural he looks here. A few months ago, I couldn't have imagined I'd let anyone into my heart again, especially not this soon. But Arjun isn't just anyone.

The messiest room needs my attention now since we're also eating in there. It's a little easier to clean knowing I'm not doing it alone and Arjun will probably have snacks waiting for me when I'm done.

It's not quick work, but the sunroom is eventually tidy and wide-open, with everything pushed off to the sides, including the couch that usually sits in the middle of the room. I wander back out to a now clean kitchen, but with the addition of a charcuterie board on the island. It's bursting with mini rolled meats, chopped fruits and veggies, crackers of various sizes, and of course cheese —white, orange, holed, soft, and hard. The board is beautiful, a swirl of colors and textures.

"I knew you'd have snacks for me."

"I made a bet with myself that you hadn't eaten yet today."

"You owe yourself twenty bucks because I had three cups of coffee, and if that's not feeding myself, what is?"

"Eat some cheese, woman."

"You don't have to tell me twice." I pop a few pieces of cheese on a cracker and shovel olives and meat slices into my mouth as my hunger finally catches up with me.

In my peripheral Arjun works on the dishes, handwashing a few items that don't fit in the dishwasher. I walk up behind him, resting my head against his back and sliding my hands around to his front, over the firm and soft muscles of his chest and stomach. I almost ask if he works out, but the memory of him chopping wood in my backyard and carrying heavy boxes of wine reminds me not all workouts are in a gym.

"Thank you for coming to help me."

"It's my pleasure. You shouldn't have to spend your birthday cleaning."

"I think that's just what happens when you get to my age."

"Oh yes, the ripe old age of thirty." Arjun wipes his hands on a cloth and turns so he's facing me. He rests his hands on my hips, pulling me flush against him. "Why don't you go get ready?"

"What about the food?"

"I told you before, I'm going to take care of it."

"You're doing way too much."

He slides his hands up my body as if it's the first time he's done it, over my ribs, my breasts, my neck, and cups my face in his hands. "I want to. Let me."

"Okay. But only because it's my birthday."

He sends me off with a kiss that leaves me dizzy.

I opt for a long, luxurious bath to treat myself, staying in the tub until the water gets cold. When I'm done, I take my time picking out an outfit and curling my long hair in loose waves. When I finally emerge from the bedroom wearing a nice pair of jeans and my favorite sweater—a lavender cowl-necked wool piece I found at a thrift store—Arjun greets me with a glass of champagne.

"To the birthday girl," he says and clinks his glass with mine.

"To me."

"Can I give you my present now?"

"I just got dressed."

"Okay, that present is for much later. I got you an actual gift."

"You didn't have to do that."

"I wanted to." He retrieves a wrapped gift from one of his bags in the kitchen, and we sit on the couch.

The box is about the size of my hand, a large rectangle. I unwrap it, revealing a navy velvet jewelry box. Placing my hand over my chest I try to contain the swell of happiness that rises in me. My eyes prick with tears.

"I know it's a little cliché to get jewelry, but this really did remind me of you," he says.

When I open the box my breath catches in my throat. Contained inside is a dainty silver necklace with a teardrop-shaped opal pendant. "Oh, Arjun. This is gorgeous."

"I noticed you don't wear much jewelry, so I got something unassuming. The opal is supposed to represent love or passion, but I guess it depends on who you ask," he says.

"Thank you." I plant a soft kiss on his lips and hand the necklace to him. Lifting my hair, I swivel, and Arjun clasps it for me.

His lips find the spot where my neck meets my shoulder and his hands skim down my arms. I shiver.

"Happy birthday, Mara."

His next kiss lands a little higher on my neck, and the next a little higher, until he's reached the spot just under my ear. I close my eyes, leaning back against him. His fingertips crawl up the edges of my sweater as he nips at my earlobe. I turn, unable to take it anymore, and crush my lips against his even as he leans back on the couch taking me with him. Just as his hands reach my ribs, the doorbell rings.

"Go away," Arjun calls and digs his fingers into my back, flattening my body against his.

I wrestle out of his hands. and when he springs off the couch to pull me back, I swat him playfully but let him pull me against him, running my fingers through his hair as he nuzzles at my neck, pressing a kiss just under my jaw.

"Hey, we have guests now."

"It's not too late to send them home."

I wiggle out of his grasp, but I suspect only because he lets me. As he returns to the kitchen, I watch the way he smooths his hair down, my heart swelling. How did I get so lucky?

"Happy birthday!" Dany shouts as I open the door. She looks like maybe she wants to hug me, but a folded-up table in one hand and a chair in the other weigh her down.

"Thank you, Dany. Are the rest of the chairs in your car?"

"Don't you dare," Arjun says as he walks past me.

I hold the door open for Dany and point her toward the sunroom. A jolt of panic strikes me. *Is any of my old artwork in there?* This is not the time or place to tell Arjun and Dany about who M. North is. I will eventually. But my exhibition is a couple months away, so I have time.

I relax when all the chairs are brought in and set up and I see that I didn't leave any of my artwork out and all my supplies are covered with a cloth in the corner of the sunroom.

"Mara, you look so pretty!" Dany squeals and hugs me.

"Hey, so do you. Look how nice you clean up." I gesture to her outfit—a blue, green, and white color-block dress, bright pink tights, and black ankle boots.

"Well, you know, finding clothes without charcoal smudges or paint spots on them is no easy task."

"Don't I know it!"

There's another knock on the door.

"Why did you knock? This is your cabin," I say to Charleigh as I open the door.

Charleigh, who convinced her family to fly up early for the holidays so she could attend my birthday dinner.

"Happy birthday, Mars Bar!" She steps inside, hugging me. I've been looking forward to this hug since our conversation almost a month ago.

"Where's Ham and Alice?" I ask.

"Alice decided a virtual BTS concert would be way more fun than her aunt's birthday party. Ham stayed back with her."

"I can't even be offended by that."

Charleigh hands me a small striped gift bag, tissue paper spilling from the top. I take it from her with a smile, setting it on the coffee table in the living room.

"Thank you, but you didn't have to get me anything."

"She said the same thing to me," Arjun calls from the kitchen. He's shaping dough on the counter with a towel slung over one shoulder.

"Mara loves gifts but likes to pretend like she doesn't,"

Charleigh says, unlayering and hanging her things on the hooks by the door.

"Oh! Gift!" Dany grabs her coat and throws it on as she runs out the front door.

"The place looks nice. You cleaned," Charleigh says, her tone teasing and impressed.

"I had some help." I nod to Arjun.

"He cleans too? Do you have a brother, Arjun?" Charleigh asks.

"How about a cousin?" he offers.

"Does he sell cheese and clean houses?"

"She's an accountant and owns three dogs," he says.

She shakes her head with a grimace. "I think I'll stick with the one I have."

"How 'bout some wine?" I ask and head to the fridge, where a couple bottles of my favorite white wine are chilling. I set out glasses on the counter, uncorking one of the bottles.

Dany walks back into the cabin, present in hand and the last guest trailing her.

"Well, I guess the party can get started now," Ethel says, announcing her presence and drawing me into a big hug.

I introduce her to Arjun and my sister. She hugs both of them, although Arjun's hug lasts longer than strictly necessary, and she gives me a thumbs-up and a wink when he turns back to dinner.

Almost every summer when I was in middle school I went to an art camp hosted by a local college. It was only a week long, but most kids struggled with homesickness the first couple of days. Not me. I practically tumbled out of my parents' van to get settled into the dorms, eager to see who my roommate would be that week. Art camp was the one time of year I was surrounded by kids who loved art as much as I did. No painting talk was too much, no one rolled their eyes when I spent extra time on a sculpture. For an entire week, I belonged.

And now, on my thirtieth birthday in my grandparents' cabin in Copper Springs, Colorado, surrounded by people who love me and people I love, I feel as if I'm back at art camp. I feel as if I belong.

"Do you want to open your presents?" Dany asks.

Everyone nods encouragingly.

I finish pouring wine into the glasses, handing them out to everyone. I set Arjun's near him and squeeze his arm before heading into the living room to sit with everyone else.

"I haven't opened presents in front of people in a very long time," I say.

"Do you remember that one birthday you—?" Charleigh starts.

"Oh my god, do not even," I interrupt.

"Now we have to hear this," Arjun says. He brings the charcuterie board to the living room, replenished from earlier, and sets it on the coffee table for us, returning to the kitchen to finish prepping the pizzas.

"This had better be embarrassing," Ethel says, delighted.

"Oh, it is." Charleigh grins.

The living room has just enough seats for all of us. Charleigh, Dany, and I squeeze onto the couch, and Ethel takes the recliner Grampy used to love.

"Okay, fine, tell the story."

"Y'all are going to love this. So it's Mara's tenth birthday, and let me just say this first: she was a very sensitive child. Cried at all kinds of things. So we're opening presents, the whole family. We were actually here, at the cabin, and Mara gets a present from our grandma. It's a small box, clearly jewelry. I think it was a ring?"

I hold up my hand to show off the silver and turquoise ring I always wear on my middle finger.

"Yes! You couldn't even wear it, right?"

"No. It didn't fit me until I was, like, in high school."

"Right! I remember now. So she unwraps the gift, opens it, and instantly starts to cry. I mean absolutely sobbing. Her tiny little body is shaking. Everyone is asking her what's wrong—is she okay? Did she hurt herself? Is something missing or broken? She can't get words out for what feels like forever, and when she finally does, all she can do is wail out 'it's so beautiful' and then cry so hard she gets the hiccups."

Everyone laughs, even me, but my face feels hot.

"In my defense, I knew the ring was super special! I saw Grammy wear it all the time and she said it was the most special ring. She told me she was going to give it to me one day. It was a very meaningful moment for me."

"Oh, that is so sweet," Dany says, still giggling.

"Got any more?" Ethel asks, grinning from ear to ear.

"I am a treasure trove of embarrassing stories about Mara," Charleigh says proudly.

"I would pay to hear a few of those," Arjun says.

"I'll give them to you for free," Charleigh offers, and everyone laughs again. "Okay, present time." Charleigh pats my leg, placing her gift to me on my lap.

I set the tissue paper from the bag on the ground, reaching in to remove the small box. Inside the box is a dainty white teacup with deep pink roses around the sides.

"This is lovely, Charleigh."

"Look inside, right on the edge." She points to gold lettering, the word "June" written in fancy letters.

"June Rose," I say, tears filling my eyes. "Where did you get this?"

"June Rose was our grandmother's name," Charleigh explains to Dany, Ethel, and Arjun. She turns back to me. "I know this sounds crazy, but Ham found it in an antiques store. He and Alice went one day after school and they found this and brought it home to me. I've had it for a couple years, but I think it belongs here in the cabin."

I reach for her, embracing her not only as a thank-you but a source of comfort as we remember our Grammy. "Thank you, seriously. This is beautiful."

"Okay, me next," Dany says.

Her present is also in a bag, albeit a much larger one. Discarding the tissue paper, I reach into the bag and pull out a frame. The frame houses a portrait of a woman looking straight at the viewer, her eyes dark with nostalgia and melancholy. There's both pain and beauty and some intangible element that makes me not want to look away.

And after a few seconds of staring, I realize this drawing is me. Fresh tears spring to my eyes.

"Oh my god," I say, breathless. "Dany, this is . . . wow. Thank you."

Arjun joins us from the kitchen. He stands next to me admiring the painting. "Wow. This is—yes. This is Mara. Can I get a copy?"

Light laughter breaks the tension in the room. Again I wipe my tears.

"There's one more gift, in the card." Dany points to the back of the canvas where a birthday card is taped. I remove it and open the envelope, two tickets falling out. I pick them up, a cold dread washing over me as I read what the tickets are for. "It's kind of a cheat," she says. "Because the other ticket is for me and this something I really wanted to do, but I'm disguising it as a birthday present."

I try to smile, but the edges of my mouth won't fully lift. My eyes are fixated on the words on the ticket.

"What is it?" Charleigh asks, leaning in as if she's trying to read the tickets from her seat.

"Two tickets to the M. North exhibition in Denver," I say. My throat feels dry and my heart is beating too hard. Everyone's eyes are on me—I can feel it. When I look up I only catch Charleigh's. She's got a calm, cool exterior, but I know inside she's all tension and questions.

"Who's M. North?" Ethel asks, breaking the silence.

I should have reacted by now. I'm making it way more awkward than it needs to be. I can tell Charleigh wants to answer the question, but that could make this more complicated. She presses her lips into a thin line.

"They're my favorite artist," Dany says. "You know that painting in the store, above the fireplace? That's theirs. And Mara likes their art too, so I thought it'd be fun if we went together. It's in Denver, just opened. They don't have any new work out—it's just a collection of their old work donated by various people for the exhibition, so the tickets were at least somewhat affordable." Dany blushes. "But well worth the splurge."

"You didn't have to do this, Dany," I tell her, not sure of what else to say.

"But you'll go with me?"

I'm tempted to glance at Charleigh. I need some support, but

166

how weird would it be to give her a look right now? So I don't. I hold Dany's gaze instead, her eyes twinkling and hopeful as my stomach knots tight. I nod, and she squeals, clapping excitedly.

"Well, mine is nothing as special as any of that, so don't get your hopes so high," Ethel says, handing me a heavy but small box.

I'm grateful for the change of topic. I already regret what I just agreed to, but how could I say no after she already bought the tickets? I stuff down all my guilt and uncomfortable feelings because right now it's my birthday, and Future Mara can deal with that.

An alarm sounds in the kitchen, and Arjun leaves us to tend to the food again.

"I'm sure it's perfect, whatever it is." I unwrap the present and open the box, carefully lifting out a ceramic cup with two tiny indents in the lip. The front of the cup has an "M" painted on it. "Did you make this, Ethel?"

"I sure as hell did. It's a water cup and the dents on top are for your brushes. I'm sure you have fancier versions of that, but I thought you might like one from your old pal Ethel."

"I really love it. This is so sweet." I stand to hug her, also hugging Dany before I sit back down. "This is really too much. Thank you, everyone," I say. I haven't felt this relaxed or happy in a long time. These people feel like my people, and the pain of this year seems light-years away.

"Dinner's ready," Arjun calls, and I shepherd everyone into the sunroom, the smells of melty cheese and baked crust making my stomach grumble. I stop by the kitchen, watching Arjun cut the pizzas and put them on serving plates. Usually in the kitchen he seems relaxed and joyful, but tonight he seems a little harried and frazzled.

"Can I help you?" I ask.

"No way—it's your birthday."

I narrow my eyes at him but leave it at that. It can be hard to host—maybe he just needs a little space. I top off my wine and carry the bottle into the sunroom, Arjun trailing me, pizzas in hand.

The table is set with the real stuff, no paper and plastic for this party. We covered the card table with a black tablecloth, and I found Grammy's old china in a cabinet collecting dust to use for tonight. It's a near-perfect dinner, everyone getting to taste each variety of pizza and declaring each flavor as the best. The conversation flows as naturally and easily as if everyone here has always been friends, as if this is a weekly dinner we have and it just happens to be my birthday. Charleigh insists on toasts, and everyone stands to give a small speech for me. I cry tears of gratitude through all of them, and no one laughs.

Bellies full and plates empty, Arjun gets up and clears the table. Everyone thanks him as he disappears, arms laden with dirty plates, only to return with a bottle of wine. He fills everyone's glasses, and I catch his wrist before he walks away from me.

"Come sit."

"In a minute," he says with a smile that doesn't fully reach his eyes. I want to say more, but Charleigh's got her hand on my arm, so I turn my attention to her.

I do my best to stay engaged with everyone, but Arjun's absence has started to bug me. I excuse myself for a moment to find him in the kitchen, cleaning. He seems on edge. I slide up to him, leaning my chin on his shoulder and wrapping my arms around his waist.

"You okay?"

"What? Yeah," he says, his voice strained.

"Why don't you come sit with us? We can clean up tomorrow."

"No, no. I'm almost done. You go back in—I'm going to bring in the cake in a few."

"But I want you in there with us. It's my birthday."

"I will, I will. After cake, okay?"

"Promise?"

He plants a light kiss on my nose. "I promise," he says without any real conviction.

But Arjun doesn't come sit during or after cake. I saw this Arjun at the cheese-and-wine event. What is he stressed about tonight though? I try to stay present, but the quiver in my stomach stays longer than I want it to.

When Ethel finally stands to leave, Dany and Charleigh follow suit. Hugs and kisses are exchanged and no one leaves without a few slices of leftover pizza and cake. Arjun helps Dany load the table and chairs back into her car, and we wave at everyone from the porch, braving the cold for a few seconds.

When Arjun and I withdraw back into the warmth of the cabin, I snag his wrist before he can go anywhere. "What is going on with you?"

"What do you mean?" His brow furrows.

I give him my best "what the fuck?" face. "Ever since you got here you've been practically frantic with activity. You barely sat down all night except for the quickest dinner known to man. My house has never been cleaner. No guests have ever had their drinks topped off so fast. This is not normal. It's not you."

"Mara, we've known each other for, like, barely two months. Not to be rude, but you don't really know what my normal is."

I flinch, recoiling, and drop his wrist.

"Shit. I'm sorry. That was—" He scrubs a hand over his face.

"Harsh."

"Yeah." He bites his bottom lip, pulling the sleeves of his sweater over his wrists one at a time. He walks past me and reaches for his jacket, shrugging it on.

"Wait—you're leaving?" I ask.

"It's not—I'm just . . ."

I grab his jacket and hold him in place. "Arjun, please. Talk to me."

His eyes flick to the floor and then back up to mine. "The thing is . . . I really, really like you, and I could see myself falling for you. When I gave you your present it just hit me like a ton of bricks."

This elicits a smile from me, and I cup his face in my hands. My heart hammers in my chest and my stomach takes the roller coaster ride of the century. "Okay . . . I don't understand why that's—"

He shakes his head, taking my hands in his. He drags them away from his face and holds them to his chest. "And that scares the shit out of me. I just started thinking about how feeling this way means I might get my heart broken again. How do I know you aren't going to wake up one day and decide I'm not enough for you?"

Until this moment, I thought there was only one kind of heartbreak: the kind that follows a deep hurt. But it turns out any number of things can crack your heart.

"But that's why I got kinda weird tonight." He trips over his words. "I thought maybe I could prove myself to you, show you I'm worthy of your love and trust."

I'm desperate to tell him he's more than worth all the pieces of my fragile, bleeding heart. He's worth more love than I have to give in an entire lifetime. The words are caught in my chest, though, snagged on my own insecurities.

Because he could just as easily snap my heart in two.

"But I want you to know that I'm not going anywhere. I'm scared, but I want to do this." He leans his forehead against mine.

I flatten my palms on his chest, feeling the thrum of his heart against my palm.

"Say something," he says, his voice a whisper. "Anything."

But I'm not sure of the right thing to say. I want to say, "Me too. I'm scared and I'm trying too," but my tongue feels too big for my mouth. So instead, I tip my chin until our lips are touching.

Arjun and I have kissed many times in the past two weeks. We've had sweet kisses and sexy ones. Kisses that led to nothing, and kisses that led straight to the bedroom. But this one is different. It's reassurance. It's healing. It's a declaration of love or passion, depending on who you ask.

As I'm tidying the sunroom after he leaves, my gaze snags on a half-finished drawing covered by a cloth. I remove the covering, taking in my work. Now it's just a vague charcoal outline of two bodies tangled together, but the vulnerability of the piece is there.

I swallow hard, thinking of Arjun's vulnerability tonight. He laid it all out, echoing the fears clanging around inside me too.

And me? I choked, unable to say the things I wanted to say or anything I needed him to hear. Now, I think of a million things I could have said in that moment. I should have said one of them; I shouldn't have left him hanging.

But every time the opportunity comes up for me to open my mouth and speak my truth, my courage abandons me and the words shrivel and die in my throat. Maybe because they know what I know: not everything is worth the risk.

Arjun seems to think this is worth the risk.

Do I?

16

There's something really strange about watching people admire my artwork without having any idea I was the one who created it. It doesn't get any less strange over time.

I hover near a table with hors d'oeuvre and champagne, clutching my champagne glass as people wander in and out of the exhibition- my exhibition- waiting for Dany to come back from the bathroom. I didn't want to be here today, and I've spent the past two weeks agonizing over my yes, thinking of ways to get out of this. But I couldn't find a way around it that didn't make me feel worse than I already do.

This is my personal hell, but it's a hell I've created for myself.

I tried to work up the courage to tell Dany the truth on the ride over, but the words dried up in my throat every time. I white-knuckled the steering wheel, trying to shove down the guilt gnawing away at me and find an opening in the conversation to say what I desperately needed to say, but I missed every opportunity.

So now I'm distracting myself by people watching, though

there aren't a lot of people at an art gallery on New Year's Eve. Someone scowls at my painting, shaking their head. Their friend nods, and they gesture. Their lips move, but I can't read them from where I am. They move onto the next painting as my insides wilt. I know my art isn't for everyone, but it's still disappointing to watch people actively dislike it.

I knock back two glasses of champagne in quick succession, wincing at the mild burn of expensive alcohol at ten in the morning.

"God, that's a nice bathroom," Dany says as she joins me, nabbing a glass of champagne for herself. "This whole place is fancy."

"It is a little fancy, isn't it?" I hadn't noticed till now while trying to see the room through Dany's eyes.

Exhibition spaces run together for me after being in so many. Some spaces are huge and echo as you walk through them. High-end spaces tend to be sparse with big windows and stark white walls. My favorite spots are the ones that feel darker, old factories converted. This space is more like one of the high-end ones. It doesn't echo, but the ceilings are tall and the walls are long and white with soft lighting placed strategically to brighten every painting and show off its colors and brush strokes.

"I'm kind of worried I'm not dressed up enough," she says with a grimace. She's paired a brown corduroy miniskirt with a cream sweater, olive-green tights, and brown knee-high boots. Her hair is lightly curled, the edges of it kissing her chin. Dangly clay rainbow-shaped earrings and a cream beret complete the outfit.

"I think you look great," I say. "Very Denver. Very artsy."

"I saw your outfit after we checked our coats and I was like 'oh shit, I am not dressy enough,' but some other people here are sort of casual too, so I'm sure it's fine." She takes a gulp of the champagne.

I'm wearing my exhibition uniform: a black bodycon dress and a pair of Louboutins, picked out by Jackie after I showed up to my first exhibition in a pencil skirt and blazer. My first big sale bought this outfit and I've had no reason to replace it. It's probably too fancy for this event at this hour, but I didn't have a lot of extra mental energy to think about my outfit.

"What do you say we look around?" I ask, and Dany lights up. She drains her champagne glass and hands it to the waiter manning the hors d'oeuvres table.

In the middle of the room are three freestanding walls, a painting featured on each side of each wall. Each of the outside walls features a single painting. Dany and I take the outer edges first, stopping at each painting.

It's sort of fun discussing my work with someone. Jackie is the only person I've ever really been able to do it with, and even then, it's nothing like this. My insides may be eroding from the guilt, but joy creeps in around the edges. I even let myself dream, briefly, of a future where Dany knows who I am and we can freely talk about my art and hers, sharing in the highs and lows of being an artist.

But that would require a level of courage I don't have. Not right now anyway. I grab another glass of champagne as a waiter passes, finishing it before they get too far away.

My guilt almost outweighs my fear. My jaw hurts from clenching it. As we round to the next painting, I steer the conversation away from my art. I need a break.

"So, how did you come to own an art supplies store? I feel like I should know this by now."

Dany's face falls a little, some of the sparkle draining from it.

"It was all I could think to do with a business degree that would satisfy my parents and still let me pursue art."

"What do you mean? You didn't want to own a store?"

"Not really. I wanted to be an art teacher or maybe get into comic books or drawing graphic novels. But my parents wanted me to be an accountant like them. The plan was for me to join the family business, but I started failing some of the classes required for an accounting major. I begged my parents to let me switch to art or education, but they wouldn't. We settled on business, and eventually I got the idea for an art supplies store."

"They preferred a business major to an education degree?"

She shrugs, staring hard at the painting we're in front of, slanting her body away from mine.

I want to tell her there's no shame in parents who aren't supportive about careers in the arts. It's all too common in this community. My own parents asked me to consider something with more stability, but they also listened when I said this was the only thing I could see myself doing.

"But you found a way around it. You teach at the store," I say.

"And I love it, I really do. Not just the teaching but owning the store. I finally have some freedom with my art. I get to draw almost as much as I want to, and teaching classes is—god, it's the best." The sparkle returns to her eyes, her cheeks flush. "And, you know, the more distance I have from college, and the more successful my parents see the store is, the better things get between us. The more accepting they are. I've been thinking about applying to this residency, actually." She bites down on a smile.

"An artist residency? Where?" I don't hide the excitement in my voice. This is one opportunity I've never taken for myself but has been on my list for a long time.

"South Korea."

"Whoa. That's so cool. But the store?"

"Exactly. The residency is six months. I don't think I could leave the store for that long. And I'd feel bad leaving my classes for so long. I don't know . . ."

Maybe it's my guilt. Maybe it's some internal moral compass buried deep inside, but I take Dany by the shoulders and look her square in the eyes.

"Apply for the residency. I'll run your store while you're gone. And teach your classes, although you may come to regret that last one."

Dany throws her arms around me. "I'm so glad we're friends," she says.

A wave of nausea hits me. I excuse myself to go to the bathroom, insisting that Dany move onto the next painting without me. I pause at the table with champagne to down a glass like a shot and slam the empty flute on the table. Once in the bathroom, I run my hands under cool water and press them, cold and damp, against my neck. I clutch the sink and wait for my heart rate to slow.

What have I gotten myself into? The pseudonym started as a way to appease a boyfriend, to feel like I still had some control over my identity as a person and an artist. I thought it would be easy to go through life the way I've been doing it for the past ten years because who needed to know who M. North is besides my family, my agent, and my partner?

And then my life blew up. But I put it back together, and now I have a friend who loves my art and doesn't know it's mine and a boyfriend who doesn't feel like he's enough for me.

My pseudonym served me in another life, but now it's a weight chained to my ankle. A wall standing between me and the people who want to love me. A shadow darkening nearly every moment I'm with these people.

I pat my hands and neck dry with a paper napkin from the dispenser, looking at myself in the mirror. There are dark circles under my eyes from lack of sleep. I've been painting again, staying up late and waking up early. I have two more paintings done, but it's still not enough, and the weight of that is written all over my face.

My hair, curled in long, loose waves at the beginning of the day, has already fallen. What little makeup I have on looks tired now, my lipstick faded, my mascara flaked under my eyelids. I wipe the black spots away, cleaning my hands off on the paper towel before teasing my hair up a bit. Lipstick on a pig—isn't that what they say?

I down another champagne glass before joining Dany where I find her at the last painting. But this glass is one too many, and I don't have enough food in my stomach to balance it out. I sway but try to right myself before Dany notices. The floor spins, and I loop my arm through Dany's, trying to make it seem more like a friendly gesture and not a "please hold me up" kind of move.

"Did I miss anything good?" I ask as we head to the door.

"All of it is good. We can go back if you want. I'm happy to look for hours. I just love their work."

"No, no, that's fine."

"I wish M. North would reveal themselves," Dany says as we walk back to my car.

The stabby feeling in my stomach intensifies. I dig through my purse and hand my keys to her. "I'm sure they have their reasons for using a pseudonym."

"Yeah . . . probably something to do with the money."

"I didn't say that." I hear the defensiveness in my tone, as if

I've left my body and I'm listening to myself talk from somewhere else. My head starts to ache, a tight band squeezing around my forehead.

"I guess I can think of a few other reasons, but if I ever put my art out there, I'd want people to know I did it, you know?"

"Yeah, but you haven't put your art out there, so maybe cut her—*them* some slack."

Dany doesn't say anything, and when I glance over at her, all the color has drained from her face.

"I'm sorry, that was—I didn't mean it, I'm just . . . My head hurts. I'm sorry."

"It's okay," Dany says, but her voice is small and mousy. The hurt in her voice is so loud tears sting my eyes.

The ride home is tense, and waves of nausea lap at me, threatening. I keep it together until I'm home and Dany has driven away, and then I empty what little contents were in my stomach off the side of the porch. I wipe my mouth, feeling slightly less dizzy but not a bit less disgusted with myself.

And then, like some kind of weird joke from the universe, a new image for a painting comes to me. A woman's face covered by a veil. The image is devoid of color, just black lines, thick and thin.

Charcoal.

I launch myself into the house, digging through my supply box to find a tin that hasn't been opened in ages. When I crack it open, the smell of every art classroom I've ever walked into hits me. Freshly sharpened charcoal pencils from Dany are in here as well as unused charcoal sticks.

I'm eager to pour all this guilt and self-loathing into a drawing, so I waste no time in getting started, only pausing to kick off my heels and shrug off my jacket in between setting a new canvas on my easel. All the tightness and pinching and aching inside of me eases with every line, every shadow, every smudge of the charcoal.

An art professor I had in college used to tell us all the time that creative work is the most vulnerable work there is. We bleed onto the canvas, show the world, and then ask them to observe it. She always said there's no real art without real vulnerability. I believed for many years that I was putting out my real, truest self with my work. I loved Colorado, and I bled that love onto the canvas. The trees and mountains and being outside—I loved it fiercely and poured all that love out into my work.

Because I loved and trusted Ben, I believed he wanted what was best for me—what was best for us—so when he made the choice for the pseudonym I agreed. But Ben didn't want me to be fully seen by the world; he wanted that only for himself. It was what was best for him, and I convinced myself it was also what was best for me. Best for us. What was a pseudonym in exchange for peace in my relationship?

But to be seen as an artist is to bare your heart and soul to the world, and my love for Colorado is just one piece of my heart. In secret I made a few paintings that showcased the rest of it. They were dark, abstract paintings that revealed the hidden depths of my pain at sharing a life with someone who emotionally abused me. And as my drawing comes together now, I recognize this art. This piece and everything else I've made in the past two months, it's full of the same truth as my secret paintings. Rife with vulnerability.

Just the thought of having eyes on these paintings, of exposing my heart and the pain inside of it, makes my heart race. Everything inside me feels weak and fluttery. I have to walk away from my canvas and drink some water to steady myself.

I am not brave enough for this, but I have an encroaching deadline, and either I continue to watch my bank account approach zero or I put my pain on display for the world. I rub my arms, trying to comfort myself. But the only comfort I find is in knowing I can put this art out as M. North.

Maybe Dany is right and hiding is a bad reason to use a pseudonym.

But if hiding is the cowards' way out, then brand me as such and court martial me. I'll stay here as long as it's safe.

17

*J*ackie is calling. Again.

Jackie has been calling every day for a week since New Year's Day, but I'm drowning in charcoal and guilt. For the past week I've been avoiding everyone. I've sent out a few texts, but mostly I eat, consume too much caffeine, and work on my drawing. I'm averaging four hours of sleep a night. My eyes feel like raisins, but every time I close my them my brain starts to formulate all the ways I can tell Dany and Arjun the truth, or of how little time I have to finish six more paintings. The upside to drowning all my problems in this drawing is that it's almost done.

The phone call goes to voicemail and I twist the ring on my finger. My phone rings again right away.

I guess I can't avoid her forever.

"What?" I answer, tapping the speakerphone button and flopping down on the couch. I rest the phone on my chest.

"You avoid my calls every day for a week and that's how you answer the phone?" She doesn't sound pissed, but she's not pleased.

"Nice to hear from you too," I say.

"Why do you sound like that?"

"Like what?"

"Like maybe you've already had a few drinks."

"It's ten in the morning, Jackie."

"I don't make judgments on your life choices."

"I'm exhausted. I haven't been sleeping much."

"Is that why you've been avoiding my calls?"

I'm not about to try to explain my self-made problems.

"I've been working on a drawing. I got sucked in by it—you know how it goes sometimes."

"Listen, are you sitting? I have some news."

"That bad?" I ask, my stomach lurching. My voice is cool and collected, but my grip on the couch tightens. The fact she didn't make any comment on how much I'm working is concerning. My brain cycles through a few options of what it could be and my heart picks up, racing in tandem with my thoughts. "Why didn't you just text?"

"This isn't text-message news. Good first or bad?"

"Bad then good."

"Everett Gerhardt called me. The Berlin location fell through for March. That's the bad news. The good news is the Paris venue had an opening, just not at the same time."

"Is this going to be a bad news sandwich?"

"The exhibition is getting moved up to February. The first."

I bolt upright, the phone tumbling from my chest to my lap. My pulse pounds in my throat and the room feels a lot hotter than it did seconds ago. "That's in less than a month."

"Three and a half weeks." She's got her agent voice on. No nonsense, no apologies. I appreciate this version of Jackie when she's working on my behalf, but I don't like her very much when she's personally confronting me.

"How long have you known?" I rest my forehead in my hands. This news is the last thing I need today.

"I've been trying to call you for a week, and I was not going to text you this news."

"You've known for a week? You absolutely should have texted with this news."

"I'm not getting into a back-and-forth with you," she says.

"I would have never said yes to this."

"Which is why I did. Because I believe you can do it. I know you can."

I'm seeing red. Even when I was painting all the time, moving an exhibition date up by any length of time was something Jackie would have run by me first.

"No, you believe it can make us a lot of money. You wouldn't have done this for a client giving us half the amount Gerhardt is."

"That is my job, Mara. If you want more say in these things you can't hide behind your pseudonym anymore."

She may as well have reached through the phone and slapped me. The room is suddenly hot and I have the urge to punch a pillow. Or a person.

"The point is I trusted you to keep my best interests in mind when making decisions about my career on my behalf, and you failed to do that. You have four paintings from me. I cannot give you six more pieces in three weeks—that is insanity. You set me up for failure by saying yes." Tears form in my eyes, a lump in my throat. "You have to call him back and tell him we aren't doing the exhibition in February and to find a date for this summer."

"I'm not doing that. I know you're upset with me, and maybe I should have called you *before* agreeing, but I know you and I know you can get the pieces together by then. We can use the commission piece as one of the paintings in the exhibition. And if you have one or two less than normal, that's fine."

"Very generous," I say, sarcasm thick in my voice.

"I'm going to let you go now. Call me if you need anything."

She hangs up, and I let out a primal scream, chucking my phone across the room. It lands with a thud on the floor somewhere far away from me.

The anger dissipates almost immediately, leaving me exhausted. I sag back onto the couch. *What am I going to do?* Even when I finish this drawing I still need to get her five more pieces in three and a half weeks. At best, I can get her one or two more.

Six is impossible.

Tears well in my eyes and spill down my cheeks. I don't know what I'm going to do. I curl onto my side, quaking, clutching a pillow to my chest.

Why doesn't Jackie see what a disaster this is going to be? What a disaster it already is. There are no two ways about it. This is the end of my career.

I must have dozed off because sometime later I jolt awake to the sound of my phone ringing and harsh vibrations against the hardwood floor. I wipe away a bit of drool on my chin and try to blink the blurriness out my vision.

The phone goes silent as I crawl off the couch to retrieve it. Two o'clock in the afternoon. Jackie called me four hours ago. I sit surveying the sunroom. It's a mess in here, and suddenly the only thing that will fix my life right now is cleaning it.

With a burst of energy, I set to straightening the room. Old dishes get stacked into the kitchen sink, blankets get folded, the floor is swept. These tasks give me something to focus on besides the news Jackie just gave me, but it doesn't really work since the deadline won't stop swirling around in my mind.

Three and a half weeks.

I survey the room for something else to distract me, because as much as I should be painting right now I don't think I could concentrate if I tried. I don't usually mind chaos, but the pressure of this deadline is threatening to crack my career, the secrets I'm hiding from Arjun and Dany are eating away at me. Everything feels out of control, and an organized space is within my grasp.

I sit in front of my art supplies: a small box and random piles of items. My hands shake as I open the box and dump the entire contents onto the floor. There's an abundance of paint tubes, an assortment of brushes and charcoal sticks, all items I've been using recently, and on top of it all, a rectangle of white paper.

I reach for it as if it might burn me, removing it from the pile of supplies with a delicate touch. It's a letter from my grandfather, the folded edges slightly worn.

In lieu of a real filing system, Grampy always used the dresser, insisting that if it was good enough for his clothes, it was good enough for his papers. After my grandfather died and Charleigh and I were cleaning out the dresser drawers, we stumbled on folders labeled "letters for the family" that contained a hand-written letter for everyone by name, including Ham and Alice.

I've read the letter three times in total. Once when I found it, and then once a year on the anniversary of his death. But this year I skipped it. I thought it might be too hard to read after the year I'd had. And I forgot until now that I'd buried it under the supplies in this box before I moved to Colorado.

I'm not sure I'm ready to read it now given the state of my life, but maybe this is exactly what I need.

My chest feels heavy as I open it, the creases giving way easily.

* * *

Mara Laine,

Your Grammy left the world yesterday, and I'm going soon too. I can't keep her waiting.

You know I'm a man of few words, but I have some things to say.

I hope you know how proud of you I am. I didn't tell you that enough. Now you can read these words whenever you need to hear them.

Don't forget to eat your greens, and remember what Grammy always said . . . if you have the choice to be honest or kind, always be both.

I love you to pieces. I'll see you on the other side,

Grampy

* * *

I can hear his voice as I read his words and I swallow a few times to try to clear the tightness in my throat. My neck is wet from where my tears have traveled past my jaw. I use the sleeve of my sweater to wipe as much wetness from my face and neck as I can before a fresh batch of tears comes with the next wave of grief.

Grampy used to say all these things to me exactly the way he wrote them here. Even when I was too old for it and I was staying at the cabin, he'd come say good night, kiss me on the forehead, and say, "I love you to pieces, Mara Laine." He was the only one who ever called me by my first and middle names, and he did in fact tell me he was proud of me every time we talked, though I'm not surprised he didn't think it was enough.

But it's my Grammy's words that cut through the fog of my crumbling career, striking me at the core and reverberating through my bones as if someone took a mallet to a gong inside me.

If you have the choice to be honest or kind, always be both.

When Charleigh and I were almost teenagers we started playing this game where we'd see who could tell the silliest stories, and then it morphed into seeing who could get away with telling the most believable made-up stories. Somehow that turned into us sneaking lies into our conversations just to see what we could get away with. It annoyed my parents to no end, but no amount of discipline would make us stop. That is until Grammy caught wind of what we were doing. One sentence from her put us in our place.

It's not a phrase she used a lot with us after Charleigh and I stopped our game, but I heard it every so often over the years, and each time I'd get a pang of guilt even when it wasn't about me at all.

What would Grammy say now if she could see the way I'm hiding from Dany and Arjun? If she could see I'm not being honest and I'm not always kind? I cringe remembering the way I snapped at Dany last week.

I thought I'd find myself after I started painting again, but I don't recognize this version of me. Would my grandparents?

I fold in on myself, shaking. Drawing my legs up to my chest, I squeeze myself into a tight ball, dropping my forehead to my knees. Unbeknownst to Dany and Arjun, we've been playing the worst game of hide-and-seek in the history of the game. I've been hiding, waiting to be caught, hoping never to be found. They have no idea they're supposed to be counting and eventually coming to find me.

The only way this game will end is if I come out of the dark.

Ready or not, it's time to step out.

$\mathcal{M}$y opportunity presents itself sooner than I anticipated. Just two days after I find the letter from my grandfather, Arjun invites me over for dinner and to stay the night. I spend most of the day working on "Girl in Pieces," never fully focused because I know what I need to do tonight and wishing time would speed up so I can get this evening over with.

I don't eat much at dinner, and although Arjun definitely notices, he doesn't pressure me to talk about anything I don't want to. And I don't. I'd rather do almost anything than have the conversation I know I need to have tonight, but I also can't stay in the dark any longer.

As we lie in bed after dinner wrapped in his sheets, my head against his chest, something stirs inside of me. Tucked into his arms, I'm blanketed in a safety I haven't felt in years. As if my body is telling my soul, this space holds nothing to fear, my chest fills to bursting, and I know if I don't say what I need to say right now I'll combust.

"I painted that painting."

"What?" Arjun cranes his neck, twisting to make eye contact, but I squeeze my eyes closed. I need to open them, and I will, but these first few words require the support of the dark.

"The painting on your wall—I painted it."

"Sorry, I'm not following . . ."

There's a question in his voice, and because I think he deserves it I open my eyes to meet his gaze head-on. *This is honesty and kindness, Mara.* "The artist who painted that painting is M. North. That's a pseudonym. It's my pseudonym. For my art."

His brows knit together as the shadow of my lies passes over him, darkening his expression. He drops his arm, scooting an inch away from me and sitting up to scrutinize me. The blankets pool in his lap, and I hold a thin sheet over my chest as I sit up.

"You're M. North? Dany's favorite artist."

I nod because the lump in my throat keeps me from forming any words. Arjun blinks a few times, stiffening as the realization sets in.

"Does she know?"

"No. You're the first person I've told in a decade. Longer," I say. The bursting feeling in my chest is gone, a weight lifted. I could almost laugh for the lightness I feel because I've done it. I've told the truth to someone! This was the hard part.

"Why tell me now?" he asks with an edge of defensiveness. "And why didn't you tell me earlier? Or Dany for that matter."

I reach out and take his hands in mine. He lets me, but he doesn't respond to the gesture. My heart shrinks. Still, I expected this. I was prepared for this question.

"Okay, let me start at the beginning. My ex, Ben, was the one who suggested the pseudonym. He said selling my art was like selling a piece of my soul. He didn't want that—he wanted me for himself. And I didn't want that, and I thought if it was important to Ben, I was willing to do it. Jackie, my agent, she didn't have any objections." I release his hands and draw my knees to my chest. This is harder than I anticipated. I focus on my ring, the way it stretches and tugs my skin when I twist it around my finger. "I never needed to tell anyone. Everyone who needed to know knew from the start. And then I met you and Dany, and I didn't expect any of this. I didn't expect to get close enough to you guys that it would become an issue. I didn't come out and say it at first because it didn't feel right, and then it just got harder and harder to say anything at all." I peek up at him.

His brow is still furrowed, but his shoulders aren't hunched up anymore. My stomach clenches. I'd pay a lot of money to hear what he's thinking right now.

"But after my birthday party, you said all this stuff about being worried you aren't enough." I reach for his hand again, and this time he meets me halfway. "And I thought maybe if I told you this, it would show you how much I trust you. That you're more than enough for me, and I'm not going anywhere."

He's silent for long enough that my heartbeat picks up. It's a drum in my throat, becoming the only thing I can focus on as I wait for him to respond.

"That actually means a lot to me. This, all of this. Telling me and why you're telling me."

"You aren't mad?"

He shakes his head. "Not mad. I don't love that you hid this, but I also understand why you did. And it was only three months. It wasn't three years."

"Are we okay?" It's a selfish question, but I can't help myself. Despite the fact he's holding my hand, only an arm's length away, he feels too distant. I want to crawl onto his lap and let him hold and reassure me.

"We're okay, but I think I need to sleep alone tonight."

If we're okay, then why am I leaving? I want to shout it, but instead I nod. My stomach dips and rocks as I slip out of the bed to get dressed.

"Are you going to tell Dany?" he asks as I'm pulling on my socks. It's not an accusation or an order, but there's no curiosity in his voice either.

"Yes. She's coming over tomorrow."

He doesn't say anything, just makes a vague sound of approval, a hum deep in his chest. Of course I'm not doing it for his approval, but it feels good all the same. I've disappointed him tonight, and even though he said we're okay my trembling limbs didn't get the message.

"And the rest of the world? Are you going to reveal your identity soon? Before or during your exhibition or something?" he asks.

I freeze for just a beat, the thought like ice in my veins. "No. I'm only telling you and Dany. There's no reason for me to reveal."

"Is it just a business decision?" he asks. Dressed, I turn to face him. His gray T-shirt is tight across his broad shoulders but hangs off the rest of his frame. Everything about Arjun is an invitation I want to accept. I would kill for a hug from him right now, but he crosses his arms as if reading my mind. A pang of regret reverberates through me. I push it away because no matter his reaction to all this, I know I've done the right thing.

Honesty and kindness.

"No, it's up to me. My agent is taking my cue."

"Okay, so what are you afraid of?"

His tone is sharp, and I rear back a little at it. I've never heard this version of Arjun.

"What do you mean? I'm not afraid of anything. It's just . . . I'm not ready," I say with almost no conviction. Saying it to Charleigh and Jackie is one thing, but saying it to a man who I swear can see straight through my soul is quite another.

"Do you still believe selling your art is like selling a piece of your soul?"

"Yes, well . . . it's complicated. It's art, and all art is putting your soul on a canvas or a piece of paper or the stage. It's vulnerable."

"But are you selling your soul by selling your art? Are actors selling their souls by selling tickets? Authors by selling their books?" he bites like he wants to leave a mark.

"No," I say weakly.

"Then why keep the pseudonym?"

I squirm under his scrutiny. "I don't know, it's just . . . it feels safe." My eyes are fixed on my socked feet, so I don't see him approach, but suddenly he's close to me, his woodsmoke scent filling my nose, hands gentle on my arms.

"Why are you hiding, Mara?"

His voice is so soft tears sting my eyes. I want to deny it. I want to tell him I'm not hiding even though I know I am. I want to accuse him of not understanding. But it seems he very much understands. In fact, he sees all the way through me.

"I told you, I'm telling Dany. Isn't that enough?"

"Maybe, but I think the world deserves to see you fully."

"I don't think I'm ready for that."

Gone is any crumb of the stronger, steadier version of myself. My courage is a battery depleted now. How do I explain to him why this is so different? Why I have enough battery to tell him and Dany and not enough to shake my career? The worst part is I think he'd understand because that's just who he is. I don't deserve it.

"I don't think I can hide with you, Mara," he says, leaning his forehead against mine.

"Why?" I jerk back, but his hands tighten on my arms, holding me to him. "Why does that matter to you?"

"Because I'm not going to spend my life trying to convince you that you deserve to be seen and known as the artist you are." His voice is gentle, and I wish he'd just yell at me—that would make this easier to bear. But he would never.

"That's not your job, Arjun. You don't have to do that."

"I know. I wish you could see yourself the way I see you, and I wish you'd let the world see you. I wish you could see how strong and capable you are, how worthy of being loved you are. But I can't force you to see your worth. I can't love you into loving yourself enough that you decide to let the world see you. But fuck, Mara, I would die trying. So I'm not going to hide with you. Because I'd spend every minute killing myself trying to convince you that you're worthy of being seen and known, and the only person who can make you see that is you. And you and I both deserve more from a relationship."

"Are we breaking up?" I ask.

He wipes away the tears streaming down my cheeks, kissing each spot on my face with an unbearable amount of tenderness. "I just need a little space, okay? Give me a week."

I nod, but the roiling in my stomach doesn't let up even after I've gone home and tried to sleep.

Eventually, I abandon sleep altogether and go to the sunroom to finish sorting my supplies. I ditched my cleaning project the other day after discovering that letter, but it gets done now, at midnight, mind racing, heart breaking.

When my supplies are organized, I lie back on the hard floor. I feel heavy. Every day, my deadline inches closer and I'm closer to watching my career tank. Being honest didn't get me anything but dumped. I hoped when I told Arjun he'd be accepting, understanding, if a little hurt. Somehow, he was all those things, and I still got called out and asked to leave.

Arjun is everything Ben never was, and I can feel him slipping through my fingers.

The only kernel of hope I have is that telling Dany tomorrow will be a positive experience. That I can get one ray of fucking sunshine in this darkness.

* * *

It's nine in the morning and I still haven't slept. I've had enough caffeine to power an army, but the painting I want to show Dany still isn't done yet. It doesn't matter that I've been working on it for eight hours—it still isn't done. Or at least, it's not right.

I stand back, studying my painting. The image came to me around one in the morning, and I never ignore the call of my muse. A halo of blue, pink, and orange surround a girl with shock-blonde hair. She's looking to the side, her hair covering her face as if she's been whipping her hair back and forth. Dany's joy and playfulness are all over this canvas. It's not a portrait, but it's more of a portrait than I've ever done. It holds some of the realism from my old pieces, but I can see the threads of my more vulnerable style in here too. I like the piece, but the thought of Dany seeing it makes me a little nauseated.

Whatever isn't quite right isn't popping out to me, and Dany will be here within the hour. As tempting as it is to cancel on her and wait until this is done, I know it's just an excuse to delay the inevitable.

I stare at the painting for too long, adding nothing, changing nothing, and then rush to get a shower before Dany knocks on my door. I have time to eat, but I couldn't if I wanted to. I have no appetite and I don't trust my stomach to keep anything down, not even the gallon of coffee I drank.

"Happy Friday!" Dany says as I open the door. She throws her arms up in excitement and then hugs me as soon as she steps into the cabin.

"Happy Friday," I say with a nervous chuckle. "Do you want anything? Water or, like, a beer?"

"It's ten in the morning," she says and gives me a funny look.

"Right, sorry."

"You said you wanted to show me something. Is it a painting? I'm so excited to see your work finally—please say it's a painting."

"Yes," I say with a weak smile. "It's a painting."

I lead her to the sunroom, my stomach rioting and my legs threatening to give out. The painting waits for us on the easel, uncovered because some spots are still drying. The reveal isn't dramatic, but Dany's reaction is.

"Holy shit, this is amazing, Mara!" Her eyes glisten, her full attention on the painting. "Wow, move over M. North—I just found my new favorite artist. And not even because this is so clearly me. Which I am deeply flattered by. Like, that was really nice of you. Is it because of my birthday gift? You didn't have to—"

"Dany." I can't take it. I squeeze my eyes closed, digging my nails into my palms.

"Oh, sorry, I get so gushy when I find something new that I love. Like when I discovered—"

"I'm M. North." I dare to squint my eyes open to see Dany's face.

She blinks a few times, her brow furrowing. "Sorry?" she asks, her voice quiet.

"You don't have to choose between your favorite artist and M. North because . . . I am M. North." I cringe.

The attempt at a joke is lame and misplaced, but Dany doesn't seem to notice. Her eyes are fixed on the painting. Red splotches appear on her neck, and her mouth twists as if she's chewing the inside of her lip.

"Okay, that was . . . Sorry," I mumble.

"That's silly," Dany says with a sort of strangled laugh. "You would have told me. You would have told me before I paid for tickets to take you to their show. Before we spent hours looking at their artwork. Your . . . artwork. Right? You would have done that." Her voice is pleading and sad. There isn't a hint of anger.

The guilt that's been living inside me is about to break free. I clutch my stomach. I'm going to be sick. "I can explain," I say. Which is the worst thing I could say at a time like this because all it does is confirm the shitty way I've handled this and says without saying it that whatever embarrassment I've put her through is justified.

Dany's eyes are wide, her brows pinched in pain, her jaw slack. She seems frozen.

"I never intended to hurt you," I say, my words coming out in a rush. "I've never had to decide if I tell people or not because until three months ago, everyone who needed to know did. Before you and Arjun I had no one to tell."

"Arjun knows?"

A stab of guilt in my abdomen. "I only just told him yesterday."

She nods slightly. The knife twists.

"I felt so guilty. I tried to tell you so many times, but I kept chickening out."

"So you just . . . let me embarrass myself." Her face crumples as if she's replaying every interaction we had. "Oh god. Oh god, I am so cringe." Dany rushes out of the sunroom to the front door. She yanks it open, and I chase after her. I don't have shoes on, though, and it's January, so I stop short on my porch.

"Dany, I'm really sorry. I—"

But she's slammed her car door and begun backing out of the driveway without a second glance.

Fuck.

19

*C*harleigh flies up within twenty-four hours of me telling her about how both of my reveals went. I texted her when Dany left the cabin to tell her everything—Arjun needing space, Dany freaking out. I told her about my new deadline and that my career is over.

The following evening, she was on my doorstep. I didn't ask her to come but didn't say no when she told me she was on her way. We're only two years apart, but even as children, when I fell and scraped my knee or someone bullied me, Charleigh was the person I went to for comfort. Our mother was always a little offended I never went to her, but for some reason Charleigh was my safe space.

The second she enters the cabin, something inside me relaxes.

With Charleigh here my cabin has never been cleaner, nor my fridge so full of casseroles. I swing between gratitude and annoyance every hour. She's not a natural caretaker—her style is more tough-love—but she forces me to get out of the house at least once a day, and to shower and have meals with her in the sunroom. It's probably good for me, but most days I'd rather bury myself in my blanket pile for the majority of my waking hours.

"I just heard from Mom and Dad." Charleigh leans on the doorframe to my bedroom, knocking lightly. I've been in bed since I woke up four hours ago, leaving only for meals and bathroom breaks. She's probably about to cajole me out of bed for a walk.

I burrow a little deeper into my blanket nest. "Oh yeah?" My voice is muffled against the layers tucked up to my nose. My eyes are closed and I regret not closing my door. I was just about to take a nap.

"Their ship just docked in Barcelona."

"Finally done with South America, huh?"

"And onto Europe. They send their love and said they'll be able to go to your exhibition a little later in the month when they get to Paris."

I grunt and roll over so my back is to Charleigh again.

The bed sags a little under the weight of her. She takes it as an invitation instead of the hint to leave that it was and places her hand on my leg over the covers. "How ya feelin'?"

"Fine," I say. A lie.

"That's what you tell me every time I ask. You know I don't believe you, right?"

I don't believe me either—it's just a lot easier to say than all the things I really am feeling. Devastated, lonely, guilty. Like there was an earthquake, but I caused it. As if somehow I reached into the core of myself and shook the fault lines inside me.

"Do you wanna talk about what happened?"

Charleigh's been itching to ask for days, and I know giving me space has been killing her.

"What's there to say? I fucked up."

"That seems like a harsh perspective on the situation."

"Okay, reframe it for me, Charleigh. I willingly deceived two people I care deeply about. I went to my own show with Dany and lied to her face, for fuck's sake." I tug the blankets over my head, the memory of my own shame too much to bear. I can taste the soured champagne in the back of my throat from the day of the show.

"You don't think Dany would have done the same thing in your situation?"

"No, because she's a good person with a good heart. And I'm a fraud and a jerk." Drained, I close my eyes, shoving the blankets off my face.

"I know you won't believe me, but Dany will forgive you. She'll come around."

"And Arjun?" I ask, daring to hope. When she doesn't say anything my heart leaps into my throat and my eyes water.

"I don't know."

Behind my sternum, there's a pinching sensation. I cough to try to get rid of it, but it doesn't let up.

"Indulge me. Do you remember my junior year of high school when I ran for student council president?"

"Of course. The posters . . . all that glitter. God."

"Yes, the glitter posters! Oh man, I wanted that so bad."

"But I don't remember you actually being on student council."

"I wasn't. Because I was asked to be the captain of the varsity volleyball team."

"Oh, I remember that. You were always at volleyball."

"Exactly, but I couldn't do both. If I wanted to be student council president, I couldn't also be volleyball captain. So I had to choose. And I chose the thing I couldn't live without."

"Don't you still play volleyball?"

"As often as I can."

"What does this . . .?"

"You told me Arjun said he wouldn't hide with you. That he couldn't be with you because he can't use his energy trying to convince you to believe in yourself." Her voice is gentle with such painful words. It almost makes them bearable to hear again.

Almost.

"So you have a choice to make. You can keep your pseudonym and your anonymity, or you can keep Arjun. You can't have both. And if you never reveal your identity to the world, I don't know if Arjun will come around." The skin around her eyes is tight, her lips pinched together.

I need reassurance right now. I need Charleigh to tell me I won't have to choose between M. North and another chance at love. Or maybe that Arjun isn't my only chance at love and someone out there will hide with me. But she can't because she knows as well as I do Arjun is right. The pseudonym is safe. Love is a risk.

The ache in my bones becomes an insufferable heaviness and I let it settle like sand in a jar of water. There's no reason to fight it. This feeling is an old friend.

Charleigh sits with me, her hand steady on my leg while I ride the wave of sorrow, fresh tears dripping onto the pillow. When the wave crashes, joining the ocean again, I wipe my face with a blanket, clearing the tears and snot, only to be left with a swollen tongue and dry eyes.

"Maybe it was all for the best. With Arjun," I say.

"Why would you say that?" Charleigh sounds personally offended.

"Because the last time I got my heart broken I couldn't paint for six months. What if Arjun and I were together for a year or two and then broke up? I lose my art again for another six months? It's probably better I'm avoiding that." Even as I say the words, I know I'm playing a dangerous game. I'm justifying why I won't take the risk of loving Arjun, knowing Charleigh will probably call me out.

"Come with me." Her tone is sharp and unyielding.

"What? Why?"

"Come on." She throws the covers off me. and I sigh. She leads me to the sunroom and points to the large canvas set up on my easel. I couldn't sleep last night, so I started working on a new piece: two bodies tangled up together. It's sketched with a charcoal outline, and I only just started on adding layers of acrylic paint to give it dimension and a more abstract look. It was both cathartic and painful to paint me and Arjun like this. Charleigh gestures to it like she's making a point.

"What about it?" I ask.

"You just said you're scared to lose your art again, that you can't paint while heartbroken. So what is this?" Her gestures intensify.

"Arjun and I were together for less than three months—I hardly think that warrants heartbreak on the same scale as when I lost my partner of twelve years. Less heartbreak, more painting." I'm digging my heels in, not really believing the things coming out of my mouth, but my lies make my reality easier to digest.

There's a spark in her eye, and I know I'm about to lose. "Look me in the eye and tell me you weren't falling for him." She squares off, challenging me.

"We barely knew each other."

"Then you'll have no problem admitting you weren't falling in love."

Of course I was, but this would be the first time I say it out loud. Maybe even the first time I admit it to myself. I fixate on my painting, avoiding her gaze. It's an intimate drawing of me and Arjun. Did I think this was just a crush? That I would feel such depth of heartbreak for someone I only liked a lot?

I cross my arms, holding onto my shoulders.

I took the leap of trusting someone again after having my heart smashed to pieces, and a measly three months later here I am again, hurting and heartbroken. The silver lining is that I'm still painting. Which means one of my worst fears hasn't come to pass. Some of the heaviness in me lifts, a burden I didn't realize was so cumbersome until it's gone.

Tears fill my eyes and my fingers itch. "I was falling for him," I say, my voice thick with sorrow. "I did."

"I know." Charleigh steps forward, rubbing my back with one hand and resting her cheek on my shoulder.

"So why can I still paint?" I ask, but Charleigh doesn't answer. "What happened back in April?" I mumble to myself more than anything. As if hypnotized, I move toward my unfinished painting, reaching for the charcoal.

Beyond the absence of her hand on my back, I don't notice when Charleigh leaves the room. The cabin could collapse around me and I'm not sure I'd realize, so engrossed am I with my piece and taking everything inside me out to weave it into this painting. All the anguish inside flows out in harsh black lines, and when I start in with the paint my shame sweeps across the canvas in dull gray, my nostalgia raw sienna, my insecurities titanium white, and my self-loathing olive green. It haunts me, not understanding why I stopped painting and why I can paint now. Why did it come back when it did? It's a connect-the-dots puzzle I can't seem to solve. I keep tracing the dots, but I get stuck, so I erase and start over, only to get stuck in a different place.

What's the difference between today and last April?

I guess for one, this time I can see my relationship with Ben more clearly than before. I know now that I ignored all his true colors for the colors I wanted him to be. I'm not to blame for how he treated me even if I can find reasons for it. I understand how love can be as hot as a fire, but if it burns and destroys it isn't love.

And maybe the most important distinction is that I'm no longer the ash and ruins of my heartbreak. Even now, tender and splintering as I am, I'm still standing.

When did that change? When did I become this version of myself? Was it after three months of therapy? Did it happen when I moved to Colorado?

I stand back from my painting, studying it and running through the past nine months in my mind, examining my memories from a distance. I watch my own life like a movie, each moment inspected for the change in me.

It was the time spent with Ashley, my therapist. Every session in which I unlearned all the toxic beliefs I held, every time she validated my emotions, and every time the scales came off my eyes about my relationship—I grew. The growth was near impossible to see as it happened, the way a tree might grow: it's planted, and after some time you start to realize it's is bigger than it used to be.

It was the road to reconciliation with my sister. I was chained and bound to the belief I'd broken us beyond repair. Learning to forgive myself, and having compassion for the abused version of me who said things she didn't mean and pushed people away when she wanted to pull them closer, set me free. Letting go of the shame of being wrong so I could apologize helped too. None of these things happened in an instant.

It was Dany's encouragement. The way she helped me draw again, sketching things when I couldn't paint. It was in her store, under her guidance, that I realized my ability to create hadn't truly left. Dany's confidence and unwavering belief in me seeped into my very soul, igniting the dying embers of my creativity.

And Arjun. Generous Arjun who pursued me even when my eyes were shut to relationships. Who saw me clearer in a matter of months than Ben did in a decade. Arjun, who cooked for me and loved to do it, who opened up to me first and paved a safe path for me to be vulnerable too. Arjun who wants me to love myself so he can love me fully.

But the changes happened at a glacial pace, and even as I pick it all apart there's no lightning bolt instance that made me who I am today. Every change in me came with time and trust and vulnerability and patience. Last April, I felt small and worthless, isolated, and sometime in the past few months all of that disappeared. I wasn't isolated anymore. I let people in again, and those people supported me. They made me feel safe and loved, and that was when I started to paint again.

My hand freezes midair, my whole body rooted to the spot. I blink a few times, trying to crystalize the understanding dawning on me.

"Hey, you okay?" Charleigh's voice breaks the spell. She appears beside me with a bowl of food, which she sets on the empty stool next to me.

I drop my arm and face her, dumbstruck. "I think I figured

out why I couldn't paint after my breakup and what happened—like, why I got it back." The words trip out of my mouth, stumbling.

"Oh, shit . . ."

"I felt so small and broken after my breakup with Ben, and I think I went blind to my own worth. Not just as an artist but a person. I lost my sense of self, and with nothing to believe in I had nothing to draw from."

"Like your source dried up? Your creativity had nothing to access."

"That! Yes. That's exactly it. Like the well ran dry. And when I started to feel supported, when I let people love me and see me and know me, I could paint again."

A fifty-pound weight lifts from my chest. I feel as if I placed the last piece of a puzzle, crossed the finish line of a race. Tears well in my eyes and I feel weak. I need support.

I sink to the couch. Charleigh sits with me.

"Mara, this is amazing. What are you going to do now?"

"What do you mean? I'm not going to do anything." What would I do with this knowledge? Wasn't the point of this just to help me understand something about myself?

"I don't know, I thought maybe this might change things with your pseudonym."

Arjun's words come back to me: *I wish you could see yourself the way I see you, and I wish you'd let the world see you.* If I do that, if I share my name and claim my art, maybe I can take back the last vestiges of me that still belong to my past.

A key slides into a lock inside me, cracking open a long locked door. Ben told me I'd be selling my soul if I did that, but what if I give it freely?

I think of my paintings in the storage shed. The style of my new paintings, my old paintings too. They say lightning doesn't strike twice, but that can't be true, because in the flash of a moment, I see the truth of my pseudonym situation and know exactly what I need to do.

I need to get to Philadelphia.

20

The parking lot of a storage space is a lonely place to be even when you have company.

The slam of the car door echoes behind me, and I adjust the gloves on my hands, pulling them a little more snugly. It smells like snow, and the overcast sky agrees with my nose. The place looks exactly the way it did in September, right before I moved to Colorado, except now, instead of red and brown leaves there are patches of leftover snow scattered across the ground.

"Well, this is a lively spot," Charleigh says as she pulls a beanie on her head. Normally, I'd throw back some banter, but being here again is sobering.

As I dig the key out of my purse I remember the girl I was the first time I was here. I'd been living in a hotel for a month, surviving on takeout and TV, and avoiding any calls from Ben and Blair. I'd finally built up the courage to ask him to be out of the house one Saturday so I could move out my stuff. I hired a moving guy to help me, and together, this stranger and I relocated my life to this storage space.

The next time I was here was four months later to pick up what I needed for Colorado. Both times I was the most broken version of myself I'd ever been.

Nothing about this storage facility has changed, but I have. Even now, reeling from a second breakup in ten months, I have things that I didn't then: healing, self-awareness, hope, my sister.

I invited her as a matter of courtesy, seeing as she has a husband and child to go home to and doesn't need to spend all her time with me, but she both insisted she'd come along and that she'd pay. And when she called Ham to talk to him about it, Ham insisted too. And now, a week after Charleigh showed up on my doorstep in Colorado, she's here with me in Philly to do this hard thing.

I don't know what I did to deserve her.

I unlock and lift the door to the unit, sunlight streaming into the space, the smell of dust and concrete wafting over me. I rented the smallest unit and still didn't even fill half of it. The two bright purple armchairs I bought from a flea market are covered in dust, one holding a pile of clothing I didn't bother to pack. I can already see that some of the shirts in the pile belong to Ben. I wrinkle my nose.

"We should have brought trash bags," I say, waving my hand in front of my face to clear the dust kicked up by our presence.

"I'll go get some. Keys?"

I hand Charleigh my keys, and when the only sound left is silence, I survey my kingdom.

My customized easel desk is piled high with the art supplies I didn't take with me to Colorado. I run my hand over one of the boxes probably containing paint tubes or brushes, my fingers leaving trails in the dust. I'm tempted to bring them all back with me now, but I can do that another time. Today is about one thing only.

I circle the space, searching. There's a stack of cardboard boxes labeled with their contents and next to it, folded up easels and a pile of blank canvases. I check around all the furniture and boxes before I find what I came for stacked against the back side of the desk: my secret paintings.

"There you are," I say, my voice small in the large space. I pick up the first one, holding it against my hips so I can take it in. It's an abstract image of a girl with her head thrown back in pain. Her face is only half-formed, the top half faded out as if she's disappearing into her pain. I remember painting this. On our sixth anniversary, Ben and I went out to a nice dinner, but he had too much to drink. He'd been drinking before dinner, drank all the way through dinner, and when we got home, he spent twenty minutes yelling at me about some paint in my hair he'd seen at dinner. Before passing out on the couch he told me how he was embarrassed to be seen with me in public, and next time to "clean up or stay the fuck at home." I remember throwing a blanket over him, getting the image of this painting, and staying up all night working on it. It was the only way I knew how to deal with what had happened.

My heart aches for me—for all the moments in my past I endured his abuse, accepting it as normal.

The next painting is a self-portrait, but all my features are blurry as if someone took a giant eraser to my eyes, nose, and lips. My hair is pulled back into a tight bun, and the background is a stark gray color. The painting is severe and disturbing. When I painted this, I remember thinking I had to erase myself to coexist peacefully with Ben.

But Ben was holding the eraser all along. Not me.

Looking at this painting now makes me realize I didn't know quite how much of me was missing by the time I left Ben. It's only now, as whole and healed as I've been in years, I can see how fractured I really was.

I flip through the rest of the paintings, each of them walking me through a distinct memory of painting them—painful memories, ones I promised myself I'd bury as deep as I could so I could continue to live the life I'd spent years building. So I could have the perfect relationship. So I could hide from the truth of my situation. I sit on one of the purple chairs with the stack of shirts, moving the clothing with my hip.

These canvases are still painful to look at. They're reminders of how small I felt, how horrible Ben was, of all the things I was feeling and not saying. None of them resemble any of the carefully curated landscapes M. North is known for. My exhibition will be a surprise to anyone familiar with my work. It's a bit of a surprise to me as well. I had no intention of being so vulnerable, but this is the art that came from the depths of me.

Landscapes give me a sense of control over my art, over how much of myself I show the world. I've been hiding in layers. Both my name and my art have protected me from putting all my pain into the world.

But I'm not hiding in these paintings. There's true vulnerability in these works. They tell distinct stories about heartache and sorrow.

And so does my new art.

These paintings tell the story of a girl trapped, believing she wasn't worthy of anything except the pain she felt. My new paintings tell the story of a girl free, healing and coming home to herself. Together, it's a collection that will display all the hidden pieces of me.

The idea of sharing it all makes me a little lightheaded. It feels as if I'm preparing to step onto a stage and get naked. If I think too hard about it, my skin gets clammy and I start to talk myself out of it. But I'm determined not to hide anymore. I won't miss out on my life.

These five pieces will complete my collection for the Paris show in two weeks. And I won't let M. North take credit for them. I want my name on these paintings. They're proof of how far I've come, of the hard work I've done to tend to my wounds and open my busted, bleeding heart to the world.

"That was the quickest Target trip I've ever—oh, hey, what's that?" Charleigh breezes back into the storage shed, trash bag in hand.

My eyes are glossy with tears.

"You okay?"

I nod, unable to form words.

She sits on the arm of the chair, peering over me to take in my paintings with a comforting hand on my back. I have the sudden urge to clutch the painting to my chest and not let her see it, but I force myself to be still. To let her see the painting. To let her see *me*.

"Holy shit, Mara. When did you paint this?"

"Six years ago."

She reaches for it, taking it out of my hands to hold in front of her. My fingers flex instinctually, trying to keep the canvas in my hands, but I force myself to let go.

"I've never seen this."

"No one has."

"Is this what we came here for?"

"This and the other four."

Wide-eyed, Charleigh follows my finger to the small stack of paintings. Her jaw goes slack and she drops to the floor, kneeling to flip through the paintings one by one, shaking her head slightly. Occasionally, she presses her hand to her mouth or over her heart. My own beats wildly in my chest, and I feel a little faint watching her take in my most vulnerable pieces like this.

"Did you paint all of them six years ago?"

"Just over the years while I was with Ben."

"And you never showed any of them to anyone? Not even Jackie?"

"Not a soul has seen them except you."

She twists to look at me, her expression full of compassion. "Are you putting these in your show?"

I nod, and when Charleigh's eyes fill with tears, so do mine. Now that she's seen them, some of the knots have loosened in my chest.

"Why now? I mean, they're beautiful and the world needs to see them. But is it just because your deadline got moved up?"

"No, although it does solve the problem of not having enough time to paint new things." I huff out a half-hearted laugh, twisting my ring around my finger.

Charleigh waits for me to continue.

I release a slow breath, undoing every entanglement inside me. "Before last April, the only way to hold onto everything in my life was to keep M. North. And now, like you said, I can't hold onto M. North and everything else. I have to let go of something, and I'd rather let go of a name than all the love the world has to offer me."

Palms up, heart open, the mask is coming off.

When I land again in Denver, I have a one-track mind. The car ride back to Copper Springs feels more like four hours than the hour and change it actually is. With Charleigh on her way home, I'm truly alone for the first time in more than a week, and for the first time since I blew up my life. I expected to feel overwhelmingly lonely when I said goodbye to her at the airport this morning, but the silence of the car and the absence of anyone else is comfortable. I savor it because it won't last long. As I pull into Main Street and park between The Artist's Outlet and the Gouda Times Bistro my stomach churns with dread, even as the hope in my chest expands the way ink spreads and blossoms in water.

In my hand, two envelopes crinkle where I grip them. Whatever financial cushion the Denver show bought me is gone, used up on two flights to Paris and hotel rooms. I want my people at my exhibition. I can do hard things without them, but I don't want to. But the confidence I had while buying these tickets is gone now, as I stare at the door of The Artist's Outlet.

I take a steadying breath and walk inside.

Someone is at the register as I approach, and I wait awkwardly for my turn to speak with Dany by the chairs at the fireplace. My painting is still above the mantle, though I half-expected it to be gone. I'm not sure I would have kept it up if I were in her shoes.

The person leaves, but Dany doesn't look up or greet me. The lump in my throat grows, but it does nothing to distract me from the pinching sensations in my stomach. I'd probably still be upset too if I were her. A part of me hoped some time and space would repair things between us, but I know that's not how this works. She deserves the apology I'm bringing to her today.

I approach the counter, fiddling with the envelopes. "I won't stay long. I just came to apologize," I say.

Dany nods, but she doesn't look up or say anything. And Dany always has something to say. Her silence is unnerving.

"I hope you know I really wanted to tell you. I was just never brave enough to do it. I'm sorry for hurting you."

She nods again but doesn't say anything.

I set one of the envelopes on the counter and slide it toward her.

She cuts her eyes to me then down at the envelope but makes no move to take it. "What's this?" she asks, her voice quiet.

"This envelope contains a plane ticket to Paris, a room for a hotel, and a ticket for my exhibition. It wouldn't be happening without you, so I hope you can make it."

The air is icy between us, an open freezer door in the grocery store. I desperately want to leave but hope Dany will accept my offering.

Her fingers dance near the envelope, but she doesn't take it. "Thanks," she says meekly, and in one swift motion she swipes up the envelope and stuffs it into the register. She turns and without a glance back at me disappears into the studio.

A cold reception from someone as warm as Dany is brutal. My ribs feel tight, and I don't catch a full breath until I'm outside the store gulping in the fresh air. I hoped that would go better than it did, but any hope I had coming here today is now shattered.

And I still need to go see Arjun.

The short walk to the bistro isn't long enough to boost my courage, so when I arrive at the store and see it's closed, I'm a little relieved. There's a notice on the door to say it'll reopen tomorrow. Maybe this is a sign I should come back another day.

No. He needs this today. Not just the ticket to my show in twelve days, but my apology.

217

I can't just slide the envelope under the door, but the idea of another cold reception makes my stomach clench. I breathe through the rising nausea and try to calm the what-if storm brewing in my mind. The cold air bites at my nose and reminds me I need to make a decision that doesn't involve standing out here all day.

I slap the envelope against my open palm and check up and down the street. A car that looks a lot like Arjun's parks in an empty space right in front of me. My stomach contracts and relaxes because this means I don't have to go looking for him, but it also means I have to see him for the first time since we broke up, and I'm not sure I'm ready for this.

But ready or not, he's walking toward me looking as stunning as ever. He's dressed casually in boots, old jeans, a black beanie, and the same puff jacket he always wears. My blood sings at the sight of him, warming me. He hesitates when he sees me—just a slight pause in his step that doesn't get past me.

"Mara? Hey. Everything all right?"

Ever the caretaker. I relax just a little. "Do you have a minute?" I ask.

"Sure, but let's go inside—it's cold." He unlocks the door, letting me through first. All the lights are off, but the sun brightens the space, and even though it's empty, the bistro feels like it always does: cozy and welcoming.

We stand just inside the door. Arjun doesn't invite me in any further, and I don't ask to go somewhere else. I need to start talking, to give my spiel, but now I'm here, so close to him, I seem to have forgotten everything I was going to say. The urge to run my hand over his cheek and feel the softness of his skin against my own is almost painful. I clutch the inner lining of my jacket pocket with my free hand to keep from reaching out to touch him.

"What's in the envelope?" Arjun shifts his weight, sticking both hands in the pockets of his jeans.

"Tickets." I blink rapidly, shaking my head a little to reorient myself. "Um, to my show in Paris. Oh, and flights and a hotel reservation. For you. And Dany too." My words stutter out of me, and my cheeks heat as I hold out the envelope to him.

He doesn't take it but cocks his head to the side and narrows his eyes in a question he doesn't ask.

"You were right. About everything." I pause to take a steadying breath. "I have been hiding. I've been hiding in my art and I tried to hide from you and Dany."

He nods, understanding. I know he isn't just listening; he hears me. I want him to reach across the space between us and hold my face in his hands, look me in the eyes and tell me he's proud of me for finally being honest with myself, but he does no such thing.

"I'm sorry I hurt you."

"Thank you."

"And I want you to know I'm not going to hide anymore." I set the envelope on the closest bistro table and head to the door but pause, turning, before I walk out. "Just one more thing," I say.

The intensity of his gaze is something I never got used to. I could spend my life receiving the full weight of his undivided attention and it would still bring me to my knees every time. Time stands still until I see nothing but Arjun. I smell nothing but woodsmoke and wine, every nerve ending in my body is on high alert, and a shiver runs through me.

I don't know why I ever wondered if this man was worth the risk.

"Letting you love me would be the best choice I could ever make, second only to loving you the way you deserve." I swallow hard and watch as every feature on his face softens. The ache in my heart flares. "I hope you'll come to Paris," I say and walk out the door.

21

*C*harleigh trades my empty champagne flute for a full one. I drink it too quickly and look to her for another. I know one of these champagne bottles costs more than my first painting sold for, but it tastes like nothing to me and it isn't taking the edge off my nerves the way I need it to.

"That was your third. I'm cutting you off."

"They aren't here yet—what if they don't come?"

"There's still time."

I haven't heard a word from Dany or Arjun since I dropped off their tickets a little over a week ago. I didn't expect to, and if I'm honest with myself I don't have high hopes they'll even show up tonight. It's a big ask, but something inside me clings to stubborn hope.

Alice runs up to us, her hands filled with hors d'oeuvres. She's the spitting of image of Charleigh at ten, with bob-length brown hair and big green eyes. My heart squeezes every time I catch a glimpse of her. I've missed three years of her life, and that's three too many. I've already been invited down for her eleventh birthday in three months, and I don't plan on missing it. Or any other holidays from now on.

"Mom, the cheese here is so good."

"It's Paris, sweetie. The cheese had better be good." Charleigh tucks a strand of her daughter's hair behind her ear.

Just the talk of cheese makes my stomach clench. I give the room another scan, taking in all the people here tonight. It's an elegant affair with black ties and gowns, updos and expensive watches. It's not my first international exhibition, but this is by far the fanciest. Everett Gerhardt's people have exceeded all my expectations. Guests of his and art collectors wander the room, clustering together with food and drink while they await the unveiling. All my paintings are covered in cloths, a small team of people hired to remove them at the right moment.

I should be more nervous than I am about the paintings I'm about to debut. About the announcement I'm about to make. But my thoughts are consumed by two people who aren't here. Who may not show.

Scanning the crowd doesn't give me the results I want, but I do find my agent.

Crisp-suited men surround Jackie holding half-empty champagne flutes and plates stacked high with miniature food. Jackie's dressed in a strapless blood-red dress with a high-low hemline and stilettos to match. She's a vision of power and elegance, and that's not lost on her or the benefactors of this event she's engaged with. Catching my eye, she raises her eyebrows. I shake my head—*not yet*—and she taps her wrist where a watch would be if the space weren't occupied by a gold cuff bracelet. I hold up my fingers: *five more minutes.* She nods and gestures back with a firm five fingers.

I nab Charleigh's champagne flute and down the liquid.

"Hey!" She grabs back her empty glass. "No more." She points a finger at me, stern and scolding.

"Aunt Mara, you can have this one." Alice holds out a full glass.

"Who gave you that drink?" Charleigh whispers sharply, looking around for a waiter to yell at. She snatches the glass from her daughter before I can take it.

Alice flashes an impish grin and races off, presumably to find her dad.

"That child is a menace."

"Doesn't get that from you," I mutter distantly without sarcasm.

"I'll take that as a compliment."

My eyes drift back to the door. Five minutes isn't a long time. New people walk in, but none of them have soft brown eyes or a head of electric-blonde hair. By the time Jackie approaches me to begin the evening I've lost all hope of them coming.

"Ready?"

"No, but I guess we can't delay anymore," I say, resigned.

"They're probably just around the corner," she says, but I don't believe her.

Charleigh gives me an encouraging nod and a thumbs-up. *Time to focus on my announcement.*

Jackie leads me to the small spotlighted area of the gallery where a microphone stand is set up. Guests start to gather closer to the microphone, including a couple of press people wearing cameras around their necks, microphones clutched in their hands. Jackie takes the mic off the stand, tapping it a few times with a manicured nail.

"Welcome, everyone. We're so pleased you've decided to join us tonight. I want to start by thanking the gallery owner and benefactor of this event, Everett Gerhardt." She mimes clapping, and the guests get the hint, clapping generously for him. "If this is your first M. North exhibition, welcome. You are in for quite a treat. If you've been to an M. North show before, you know me— I'm Jackie, M. North's agent and manager. This is usually where I tell you a bit about the exhibition, but—"

The door opens, and a gust of wind followed by footsteps echoes into the large space. Every head turns in the direction of the newcomers.

My heart drops into my stomach then jumps up to my throat.

"Sorry," says a voice I recognize. It belongs to a girl with hair the color of sunshine. She garners looks of disapproval in her lavender faux fur coat, pink tulle skirt, and gold glitter sneakers.

I pinch my arm to make sure I'm not dreaming. Dany, accompanied by Arjun, sweeping a few minutes late into my Paris exhibition. Tears pool in my eyes.

Arjun sheds his peacoat, handing it to a gallery staff member, revealing a black suit that looks so good on him my mouth goes dry and I forget where I am for a second. His beard and hair are neatly arranged. He looks incredible.

They came to Paris.

"But tonight," Jackie continues, and the all the attention in the room snaps back to her, "I have a special treat for you."

This is my cue.

Jackie hands me the microphone, and I tear my eyes from the new arrivals. Accepting the mic, I take her place in front of the stand. Murmurs rise through the crowd, cameras click in quick succession, and I clear my throat, smoothing my dress over my thighs.

"Good evening. My name is Mara West, but you know me as M. North."

A few people gasp and the murmurs turn to chatter. Heads swivel as a thousand photos are taken. I take in the crowd for a moment, but my eyes land on Arjun. There's a slight smile on his face.

"When I sold my first painting, I chose a pseudonym because it felt like the only way I could give my art to the world and still feel like myself. But the past ten months have been eye-opening for me. For nearly eight months, I had the worst case of artist's block I've ever experienced, and when I did start painting again, I barely recognized my own work. The pieces you're going to see tonight are very different from what you've come to expect from M. North, and this is why I'm telling you who I am. Because the art you're seeing tonight was painted by me, Mara West. This work is more vulnerable than anything I've put out before." I clear my throat, swallowing hard. My whole body trembles, and I suddenly wish I weren't up here alone. My eyes sweep across the crowd, landing on the smiles of my support system. The pride on their faces bolsters me. "Five of the pieces you'll see tonight, the ones on this half of the room,"—I gesture to the left side of the room—"are pieces I've created since October, inspired by people who believed I was brave enough to do this tonight. The pieces on this half of the room"—I gesture to the right—"were painted many, many years ago. They've been sitting in storage because I swore I'd never show them to the world. They were too vulnerable, too personal."

The clicks of a camera fill the silence of my pause. I lock eyes with Arjun.

"But I'm not hiding anymore. This is me, and this is my art. Thank you for your support. I hope you enjoy."

Jackie nods to the team standing by to unveil my paintings and the cloths come down. People clap, and the photographers come forward asking for a photos of Jackie and me and just me. Questions are volleyed at me, and Jackie assures reporters I'll be happy to schedule interviews in the coming weeks. It's a frantic few minutes as I try to keep up with the congratulations and handshakes from foreign faces. Jackie shoos them all way, accurately reading my overwhelm. She leads me off to the side where Charleigh, Ham, and Alice are waiting for me, and promises to take care of the press.

"You did amazing. I'm so fucking proud of you," Jackie says.

I'm still shaking from the adrenaline, and when Jackie pulls me into a hug I cling to her for an extra second, needing the time to compose myself. She gives my shoulder a squeeze and then leaves me to my sister.

Charleigh throws herself at me with a ferocious hug, and some of the tension in my chest eases. My pulse pounds in my ears. I remind myself this is excitement, not anxiety, and let the comfort of my sister's embrace bring me back to myself.

"I know you're probably sick of hearing this from me, but I'm so proud of you. Seriously," she whispers in my ear. When she leans back she holds my shoulders, her eyes sparkling with tears. She hugs me one more time before letting Ham and Alice have a chance to hug me too. They shower me with praise until Dany steps into my peripheral.

My sister and her family give me the thumbs-up and big smiles as they back away.

"You came," I say, turning to Dany.

"Well, you are my favorite artist," she says as she steps up to hug me.

"I'm sorry, Dany. I had no intention of hurting or humiliating you." I hold onto her arms after our hug, holding her eye contact.

"I know, and when I got over the embarrassment of how

cringe I was with you, I think I was just left with hurt. I wish you trusted me enough to tell me."

"It wasn't that I didn't trust you. I didn't trust myself to be vulnerable with you. It wasn't you at all. It was me."

She nods, understanding. "And now?" she asks.

"Now, well . . . you did say the first time we met that we were going to be friends, so I hope that's still true. But this time I won't hold anything back."

Her eyes shine, her smile stretching from ear to ear. She hugs me again, and I don't hold back the tears that come with the wave of gratitude. When Dany release me she turns me around by the shoulders to where Arjun is standing, hands tucked casually into his pockets. My stomach flips, and Dany gives me a wink as she walks away.

"Show me your favorite piece," he says.

I take him to the charcoal/acrylic painting I did after our breakup, titled "Bodies." Hurting as I was, I poured all of me into this. All the things he made me feel, all the ways I came alive when he was near me. It's an intimate piece, but I never considered not showing it.

"Do you like it?" I ask.

"I love it." There's awe in his voice, and my heart drops into my stomach.

"It's yours if you want it."

The way he looks at me feels as if he's reached his hand into my chest and claimed my heart for his own. He turns toward me, closing the gap between us. Every cell in my body cries out for his touch, so when he trails his finger across my cheek to tuck a strand of hair behind my ear my legs turn to jelly.

"I thought I could see you before, but this . . ."—he gestures around the room—"has shown me I only knew a small part of you. I feel like I understand you now in a way I never could have done without these pieces. You—the truest, most honest parts of you—are all over these paintings. So, actually, I want all of them." His voice is low, traveling through every inch of my body.

My breath catches in my throat. I bite my bottom lip, hope swelling in my chest like a sponge, absorbing the way Arjun looks at me and the feel of his hand against my jaw and neck. Somehow, his woodsmoke and wine smell is here even after traveling all those miles.

My skin feels hot, and I take his hand in my own, placing a soft kiss on his palm and pressing his hand to my cheek. Everything fades but us. The people disappear, the gallery blurs, and all I see is Arjun. "Thank you," I say.

"For what?"

"For making it safe enough for me to come out of hiding, to show the world all of me. All the lovely things and the shattered, ugly pieces."

Arjun touches his forehead to mine, slides his hand to the back of my neck, and kisses me the way I hoped he would. "I love all of those pieces," he whispers against my lips. "I love you."

"I love me too."

I feel him smile and circle my arms around his neck. Then I kiss him until it's absolutely clear I love him too.

en months later . . .

The knock at the door is the last guest.

Charleigh and her family are all here, Mom and Dad left earlier today to hop on their next around-the-world cruise ship, and Arjun was here before everyone since he lives here, but we're missing one guest.

"Door's unlocked!" I yell, hoping she'll hear me through it. My hands are tied with reloading the wood stove, and everyone else is busy getting ready for the feast.

"Sorry I'm late," Dany says as she walks in, casserole dish tucked under an arm.

"You're not late. The boys are still fiddling with the turkey, so you're fine," I say, dusting off my hands to hug her and take the casserole. I set it on the kitchen island while Dany hangs up her jacket and scarf and leaves her boots with the rest of the shoes by the door.

Since my show in Paris, Dany has become one of my closest friends and biggest supporters. Though I haven't had a creative block as bad as the one that lasted eight months, I've had a few, and Dany gets me through them each time. She feels more like my partner in creativity, and our friendship has become everything I'd hoped it would be.

"Are you getting excited for your residency?" I ask.

"I don't even leave until January first."

"So is that a yes, you're basically dying inside?"

"I mean, it's only thirty-six days away, but who's counting? Not me. By the way, can you believe we got snow on Thanksgiving?" She joins me in the kitchen with a hug.

I introduce her to Hamilton, and she hugs Arjun after sneaking a bite from the charcuterie board we've all been picking at today.

"Alice was very excited about the snow," I say.

"Snow is always exciting," Dany says, and I know better than to argue.

She and I head to the sunroom where Alice and Charleigh are setting up the table. Beyond just plates and utensils, Alice has decided each setting is getting a handmade craft.

A girl after my own heart.

Dany volunteers to help with enough enthusiasm that Charleigh deems six hands too many and loops her arm through mine, dragging me out of the sunroom and into the kitchen. I relish the short walk with just my sister. Since last fall, we haven't had as much one-on-one time except for our almost daily FaceTime calls. There's been a ton of family time and birthdays and holidays celebrated. We've probably made up for all the lost time, so now we just get to enjoy each other, burn marks and all.

"It's wine time, dear sister," Charleigh says, digging through the cabinets for wineglasses and a bottle opener.

I take the opportunity to slide up to Arjun, looping my arms around his waist.

He plants a kiss on my forehead. "Can I help you?" he asks, pausing to wrap one arm around me. He's careful not to put his hands, which are covered in some kind of seasoning and oil, on me.

"Just feel like you've been so busy today."

"Dinner won't cook itself."

"It should."

"Should we petition NASA to make a robot that will make us dinner?" Arjun says, his smile lighting up his face and making my knees weak. Nearly a year together and he still has this effect on me. I thought it might fade, especially after he moved in with me this summer, but if anything it's become more intense the more I fall in love with him.

"Just the one? Seems selfish," I say.

"Guess you'll have to deal with me trading time with you for time in the kitchen then. Unless of course you want to help."

I scrunch my nose at him, and he pecks a kiss on the tip of it. "I think we both know that's not a good idea," I say.

"I'm happy to teach you—you know that."

"You have the patience of a saint. And the kindness of one. When you die, we'll put your face on a candle and a necklace."

"A little morbid for Thanksgiving, but I'll take it." He kisses me, a quick peck on the lips, but it makes me wish we were the only ones here, that we didn't invite everyone up for the holiday and had the cabin all to ourselves.

But I was the one who came up with the idea. Thanksgiving

has been lonely for many years—even last year, when I was surrounded by people who loved me but I had no idea how to get out of my own pain and guilt to let them. This year, though, I resolved to use this holiday as a way of celebrating how far I've come.

"Did you hear back from Jackie?" Charleigh asks as she hands me a wineglass.

"It's a holiday," I say.

"Has that ever stopped her?"

"Fair point. But no, I haven't heard. She said it could take a couple weeks. I might not hear till mid-December."

Everett Gerhardt was indeed pleased with my exhibition in February and his custom piece, and this past summer I filled three of his galleries with exhibitions. Most of the pieces have sold already, but one in particular is caught in a bidding war. Jackie told me last week and said she'd call when she had news, but not to get my hopes up about anything final for a while.

"What's the piece that's up for auction again?" Charleigh asks.

"It's called 'The Mask.' It's that massive one of the venetian mask, the blue-green abstract one?"

The painting is massive, eight feet long and five feet high. It took me months, but it was a labor of love and healing. It's the sort of mask that covers the eyes and bridge of the nose, but in my painting only half of it is intact, the other half shredded, pieces swirled in abstract lines and shapes.

"Oh yeah. I loved that one. Out of my price range though," Charleigh says with a wink.

"Dinner's ready," Hamilton announces, and we all gather in the sunroom for our meal.

It's my first Thanksgiving in four years that I'm not eating a microwave meal in front of the TV. It's overwhelming being surrounded by this much love, but for the first time since my grandparents passed, this week has been entirely bearable. There's been grief, but there's also so much support.

Had someone told me a year ago this is what today would look like, I might have rolled my eyes. But here I am, healed and still healing. Putting my art out as Mara West. Loving again and being loved in return.

It's been one hell of a ride.

I already warned everyone I'd be making a speech, so when our bellies are full and hurting from laughter I stand, my chair scraping against the hardwood. "Okay, I warned you guys this was happening. This past year, I—"

Arjun stands too. I give him a "what the hell?" look, but he digs in his pocket and then suddenly he's kneeling, holding a small box in his hand, and multiple people squeal and clap.

"This past year you've grown so much. I have loved being by your side as you navigate your career and the whole world knowing you, watching you put out art that shows everyone who you really are, which is someone I love very much."

"I love you too," I say, my voice wobbly, tears already forming in my eyes.

"And I want to continue to be by your side for all of it. I want to be your arm candy at all your shows and cook you meals when you forget because you've been painting for hours on end, give you back massages when you're sore from hunching over a drawing . . . I love everything about the life we've built. I love to see that glazed look in your eyes when I start telling you the finer points of a Havarti, when you surprise me at the store or leave doodles on sticky notes in my car and the food in the fridge. I want this forever. I want you forever. Will you marry me, Mara Laine West?" He opens the box, revealing a gold vintage ring with a perfectly round diamond in the center.

It's the easiest yes I've ever said.

ACKNOWLEDGMENTS

Writing is a solitary hobby, but it doesn't have to be lonely. The time I spent on this book was never spent alone. The support from my community is the reason this book is in your hands today.

My first thanks is to my writing wife and critique partner, Sheila. This book would not exist without you. I would probably be a pile of self-doubt flavored goo if it wasn't for your tough love, encouragement, card pulls, and check-ins. Thank you for loving this book and my characters as much as I do and for carrying me through the darkest and brightest spots of my writing journey.

This book wouldn't be what it is today without my team of beta readers who not only gave me honest and thoughtful feedback, but also cheered me on. Thank you Heather, Ana, Julie, and Kate. (An extra special thank you to Julie for her feedback and knowledge on all things art!)

Speaking of feedback, I am the writer I am today because of a handful of other writers who critiqued my early chapters of this story and helped shape it into the story you just read. Thank you Josh, Laura, Kat, Kate, Becky, and Marissa. Your endless support through this process has

Mallory, for creating the most thoughtful book cover in existence. What an honor to collaborate with you and have your art out in the world with mine.

A huge thank you to my editor, Bryony. Thank you for believing in me and loving my story. Working with you has been an absolute dream. You elevated my writing with your eye for detail and your red pen, and I am so glad we live in a world where I could find you and work with you! And an extra thank you for the proofreading help, for going over and above on edits when crisis hit.

To my husband, Allen, who never complained about a single hour I spent away from him to work on this book, who only ever believed in me and enthusiastically insisted I get this book out into the world... thank you. I love you.

My unending gratitude to my friends who cheered me on and celebrated every step of the way, and to my family for their support and enthusiasm.

My last thank you is to my NaNoWriMo region for loving Arjun and Mara before anyone else did. This pants magic never would have happened without you guys.

A NOTE ABOUT THE COVER DESIGN

My incredible cover was designed by a dear friend and talented artist, Mallory Michael. Each item and paint color on the cover were specifically chosen to represent moments and larger themes in the story. Mallory wrote me a note explaining her choices when she sent me the cover, and the level of detail brought me to tears.

After reading the book, some of the elements on the cover might be obvious to you, such as the charcoal sticks, but I hope these notes from the cover designer herself give you a deeper appreciation for the artistry and thoughtfulness of the cover design.

The ruined flat brush with green paint represents Mara's failed attempts at painting and showcases Arjun's favorite color.

The deep red/purple is for the wine Mara and Arjun share together.

The yellow paints is for the color of some of the cheeses within Arjun's shop.

The blue on the larger paintbrush and the palette is for the blue balloon Mara paints on Arjun's cheek.

The palette knife represents Mara's palette knife and her wins and losses with it in hand.

And lastly, a blank canvas for Mara's new start and new love for herself.

ABOUT THE AUTHOR

Liz Leiby is an emerging romance author. She holds a bachelor's degree in theater from Birmingham-Southern College and lives outside of Philadelphia, Pennsylvania with her husband and two cats.

When she's not writing, Liz likes to bake, lift weights, garden, hike, and read. She hates ketchup and season 8 of Game of Thrones. Her dream is to travel to New Zealand one day.

This is Liz's debut novel.

CPSIA information can be obtained
at www.ICGtesting.com
Printed in the USA
BVHW030801081022
648778BV00003B/12